THE LOST LIFE

STEVEN CARROLL

THE LOST LIFE
A NOVEL

FOURTH ESTATE • *London, New York, Sydney* and *Auckland*

Fourth Estate
An imprint of HarperCollins*Publishers*

First published in Australia in 2009
by HarperCollins*Publishers* Australia Pty Limited
ABN 36 009 913 517
www.harpercollins.com.au

HarperCollins*Publishers*
25 Ryde Road, Pymble, Sydney, NSW 2073, Australia
31 View Road, Glenfield, Auckland 0627, New Zealand
1–A, Hamilton House, Connaught Place, New Delhi – 110 001, India
77–85 Fulham Palace Road, London, W6 8JB, United Kingdom
2 Bloor Street East, 20th floor, Toronto, Ontario M4W 1A8, Canada
10 East 53rd Street, New York NY 10022, USA

National Library of Australia Cataloguing-in-Publication data:

Carroll, Steven, 1949–
   The lost life : a novel / Steven Carroll.
   ISBN 978 0 7322 8480 0 (pbk.)
   Eliot, T.S. (Thomas Stearns), 1888–1965 – Fiction.
A823.3

Cover design by Sandy Cull, gogoGingko
Cover image by Jessica Marcotte / Jupiterimages
Internal design by Alicia Freile
Typeset in 11/18 Baskerville BE by Kirby Jones
Printed and bound in Australia by Griffin Press
70gsm Bulky Book Ivory used by HarperCollins*Publishers* is a natural, recyclable
product made from wood grown in sustainable forests. The manufacturing
processes conform to the environmental regulations in the country of origin,
New Zealand.

5 4 3 2 1   09 10 11 12

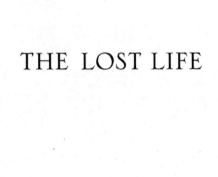

THE LOST LIFE

PART ONE

The Rose Garden
Early September, 1934

On a bright autumn day, in the early afternoon, two young people set out to cross the mile or so of open sheep country that lies between their town and an estate nearby that is rumoured to have pools. The day is at its hottest, and Catherine, who carries a bag containing togs and towels, is ready to throw herself into the water without changing if the rumours prove to be true. The sounds of sheep are all around them, even when there are no sheep to be seen. The occasional bull gives them a menacing once-over, but her companion, Daniel, walks across the fields, as if the sheer confidence of his stride is sufficient to render all property communal – he, Catherine, the sheep, the cattle, the birds that are perched in the shade of the trees, farmers, tradesmen, students and lords alike all share the land together, and the cattle, detecting no sign that the young man feels out of his territory, leave the couple alone.

Out here they are free. No small-town eyes. They pause and kiss. Often. Long, aching kisses. They walk on, their faces, their skin, hot from the day, the walking and the kissing. They have come this way as much to be alone as in search of cooling pools. But the pools would be nice, convenient even. Instead of just undressing in front of each other, which they have never done, they would be bathing together. Bathing is good like that, gives you a *reason,* she thinks, as she tramps along just a bit behind. Lets you get undressed, or almost. People get about when they're bathing as they never would on the street. Yes, pools would be nice.

They enter the estate gardens through a fence not far from the long, winding driveway. Strictly speaking, this is trespassing. But Daniel isn't hearing any of this either, for it is known that the house is unoccupied and has been all year. Catherine follows. He is, after all, four years older, and knows his way around.

The old wooden gate slowly closes behind them and they pause where they stand, Catherine noting that this would be the perfect place, later in the day, to watch the sun set over this part of the Cotswold Hills. They stroll on, and those few paces transform the afternoon. The vegetation is suddenly dense. The leaves are thick on the trees, the earth is soft, almost moist, and the air is cool and soothing. But, more than this, there is the feeling of entering the storybook world of children's tales as removed from the ordinary world as Catherine and Daniel are now from the drowsy heat of the autumn sun. It is by pure accident that they haven't entered the property through the driveway. They have no map, but know generally where the place is, and have happily stumbled into it their own way. Had they come along the driveway there would have been no sign telling them the name of the place. All the same, they know this is Burnt Norton.

An odd name for a house. But its history, of which the locals are vaguely acquainted, is also odd: a history of dissolute barons, drunkenness, loose women, madness and whatnot. Whether by drunkenness, design, or drunken design, the original house had burnt to the ground centuries before and the new one was named after it. And, to an extent, it isn't just the promise of the estate's pools (however murky they may be) that has drawn Catherine and

Daniel here, or the chance to be alone; it is also the place itself and the lure of a bit of local colour.

Now, the leaves dappled, the sun bright, hidden, then bright again, it is the storybook strangeness of the place that Catherine is registering, as much as the cool, soothing air around them. And while she is staring up at the dappled leaves and the canopy of branches above her, she feels Daniel's lips on the back of her neck, and she smiles, but gives him the slip. Ardent, that's what they are. Two characters in a novel she read the day before were ardent, and she thought, yes, that's us too. 'Ardent' was their word – although she hasn't told him yet. It's a good word, and a strong one too. And so when his lips touched her neck, she thought 'ardent', then slipped out of range of his lips and his arms and grinned.

When they finally wander out from this thickly wooded part of the estate and onto one of the house's many lawns, glumness falls across their faces. There, before them, is the rumoured pool. Drained. Without the prospect of watery relief, Catherine lets out a slow groan as she touches the pack containing their togs and towels and communicates her disappointment to Daniel with a roll of her deep brown eyes, the same deep brown eyes that he has gazed into all summer long without once tiring of them. He shrugs his shoulders. She, hers in return. What can they do? There is the pool for which they came, directly in front of them. Drained. And, what's more, it has clearly been drained for some time. Its edges are brown where the summer sun has dried the moss. As they stroll slowly around it, the sun, which had gone behind a small cloud, bursts upon the open, blue sky and hits the bottom of the circular concrete pool, creating a blinding glare. And, for a moment, it seems as if a miracle has happened: that the heavens have filled the pool for their pleasure and their use alone. As Catherine stares into the dazzling spectacle (but not for long because the light is blinding), she feels as though she might just be able to dive right in and drench herself in the element of air instead of water. Then the sun goes behind another small cloud and the pool is no longer filled with sunlight, but is simply drained and empty, as drained of sunlight as it is of water.

They walk on, cross the lawn, and there are two more pools, but their hopes are dashed again as soon as they look at them. Drained, both of them, and, with no more clouds in the sky, the sun is in its early-afternoon ascendancy, and the day seems hotter than ever. Catherine gazes upon the larger of these two pools, a long, rectangular affair, and imagines propelling herself, dolphin-like, end to end, until she is cooled to her bones and exhausted. But there will be no such swim. Nor, she realises, will they be permitted that moment of discreetly disrobing behind bushes somewhere, slipping into their togs and getting a good look at each other because they would be bathing, after all, and looking is allowed. That would be disrobing with a purpose. But without the purpose, without a *reason*, they have no excuse, and the world requires an excuse before it can give you permission. Presently, they pass between the two pools and out into the rose-lined aisle that leads up to the house.

Pruned rose bushes stand like servants either side of them as they walk up the crumbling path to the red-brick arch at the end of it; path, shrubs and wall, all daubed in sunshine and shadow; the feeling, like stepping into and strolling through, an impressionist painting. Catherine, having cast off the disappointment of the drained pools, is now gliding up the aisle, lulled by the abundance of greens, pinks and reds all around her, while Daniel follows a pace behind her, more intent on the figure than the landscape.

Then they are under the archway and out into the rose garden. There are hedged squares of roses, white and pink, all around them, and as they come to a stop she turns to him, eyes alight, as if to say, hang the pools, we've got this. All of this, she sighs, and no one to see it. A shame. But the thought has no sooner passed through her mind than she concludes it is as it should be. The property is unoccupied, there are no gardeners about, and this is a private viewing, all the more thrilling for being so. She imagines that the flowers are greeting them, as guests, welcoming these two young people into their home. But of course they are not. This is what her books of literary criticism and critical terms (at eighteen, she is preparing for her final year of school, a childhood illness having kept her from starting school until a year after everyone else) call the 'pathetic fallacy'. No, the rose bushes are not gracious hosts, and Catherine and Daniel are not their guests, and the flowers are not inclining towards them as if to greet them. That is just the length of the stalks and weight of the blooms bowing to gravity, if anything. To invest these flowers with human characteristics, as having the manner of hosts (and gracious ones at that), is to indulge in the pathetic fallacy. Flowers are neither happy nor sad nor gracious nor rude, and sunsets pass without melancholy on the part of the sun or on the hills behind which it nightly sets. Nor do the trees and flowers or, indeed, this country house itself require human eyes and emotions to see the days through. Nor do they need to be observed by human eyes in order to exist. They simply are, thank you very much. And she smiles at that. For, in spite of her literary texts, the insistence of Mr Ruskin (who coined the term), and her awareness of the pomposity of the pathetic fallacy, she is aware that she has been talking to the flowers, and the flowers have just answered back.

Soon they are lounging on the lawns at the front of the house (obviously trimmed and well-maintained by absentee staff). She opens up her pack and takes out two cheddar sandwiches. Daniel carries the weightier objects in his pack, two bottles of beer wrapped in wet newspaper to keep them cool. She'd never drunk beer until this summer. Cider, yes. But she's getting a taste for beer. Daniel likes his beer and insists on getting two bottles when they go walking. It is accepted that she will only drink half of her bottle (as she always does) and so he downs his smartly, knowing that another half is still waiting to be savoured. And, although the local brew isn't particularly strong, the combination of sun and beer makes itself felt almost immediately.

Daniel, who was born and raised in the town, is back from Cambridge, Downing College, as he is every summer. Only this is the last time he will come back for the holidays in quite the same way. He has finished his degree and will soon, at the end of autumn, leave for Paris to study more, and, quite possibly, just lounge about. He has, his father (a shopkeeper in the town – greengrocer and small goods) maintains, picked up bad habits at the university. He'd left the town a sensible lad (albeit one known for being a bit of a prankster and a dare-devil), and come back at the end of that first year proclaiming himself a Marxist. Marxist, in his father's mind, was nothing more than fancy talk for troublemaker. And he hadn't spent the last twenty-two years bringing up his boy (the last twelve by himself) to be a troublemaker – whatever toffy way you might find to say it. Daniel told his father that half the university was Marxist. Marxism was the future and it worked, he told his father. And his father replied that it might be the future but nobody in it worked. This new way of looking at the world and the laws that governed it was apparent in everything Daniel said and did. And so it was no wonder that he strode through the countryside, as he had an hour before, in a way that suggested to all forms of animal life around him that the world belonged to everybody. He was, as it were, ideologically equipped for just such a stride and just such a manner of walking. A manner of walking that, in its very assertiveness, was a political act.

Catherine is originally from Broadheath, just outside Stretford, her mother a school teacher who had come to the town only the year before. Her father, who had defied family tradition and not gone to the mills but joined the merchant navy, had set off on a voyage to India when Catherine was two-and-a-half and never come back, even though he'd told her mother often enough that she was beautiful (too beautiful for him) and he was head over heels in love with her, and that he could never live without her. Intermittent cheques arrived in the post from various parts of the world, until they ran out with a letter telling his wife what proved to be a cock-and-bull story about being held in some jail in Calcutta. Two years later (the war over) he was seen by her mother's sister promenading through a park in Manchester with a new suit and a new girl. Together, mother and daughter have now lived in various parts of the country, but this town, her mother says, is the final stop.

Daniel is twenty-two, Catherine eighteen. But, he freely acknowledges, she knows just as much about life, and neither of them feels the age difference. He'd escaped the confines of the town to university, where, instead of discovering the intricate structures of Elizabethan songs, sonnets, rondels and running rhymes, and the kingdom of individual experience they communicated (as he thought he would), he discovered, through reading Mr Marx, the impersonal iron laws of History, laws that united all private lives on Earth as surely as the laws of gravity kept everybody's feet on the ground – or ought to. The world, he was happy to tell Catherine and anybody in earshot, was falling apart and thugs were rising from the rubble. This was no time for poetry. She agreed the world was falling apart (you only had to look at the newspapers) and that thugs were rising from the rubble, but she didn't see why you had to throw out the poetry. Byron didn't, she said one day, and that shut him up for a moment.

Daniel had escaped the confines of a small town, she'd told herself all summer, and the very next year she intended to as well.

And, as much as the town might have suggested that they started hanging about together because she had no father and he had no mother (Daniel's mother had died with the flu when he was ten) and that they were united by private grief, the fact was they just liked the look of each other. Neither of them was dismissive of this or held it to be a superficial attraction; in time they both agreed that the things people like the look of tell you a lot about the people themselves. For they both had a certain kind of look: something out of kilter with the age. No fashionable clothes (for all his talk about the 'future', Daniel was strictly old world to look at), and she practically no make-up and possessing none of the graceful, flowing dresses that actresses wore on the screen, off-the-rack imitations of which girls wore on Saturday nights to make themselves look like actresses. But it was more than that. They both projected a kind of conservatism, a social conservatism that masked the rebel in him and the hunger for life in her. It was no surprise to either of them that they agreed on many things: politics, books, the town and just about everybody in it. And even when they disagreed, they were united by a shared passion to do so. The only books worth reading, he'd say, were the ones that shook the world up. By this he meant, of course, that books – poetry, novels and, yes, the bloody doddering theatre – had to be political in some way. No, no, no, she came back at him, again and again. Too simple – a charge that Daniel took calmly and happily because he knew they were both on the same side. Poems, novels, stories, Catherine would say (and Daniel from the start admired her confidence, a confidence beyond her years), give people the lives they will never live and fill them with a yearning for something else, something more. A way of living in the world that doesn't yet exist. Doesn't yet exist but dreaming about it just might make it so. And books that speak about these things just might make it so by inspiring people to go out there and *create* their lives, not have their lives imposed upon them. Isn't that shaking things up? Why do you think mothers and fathers and nuns snatch novels from the eager hands of girls of a certain age? Because they might get ideas – and we don't want that, do we? And why do you think fathers snort at the sight of their sons with their noses stuck in books? Because they might just get above themselves, and what was good enough for them and their fathers and their fathers' fathers – the mills or the mines – won't be good enough for their sons. And even though Daniel always felt there was just a bit too much of the Rugged Individual about all of this, he still couldn't help but be swept up in her sheer enthusiasm – that and the sparkle in her eyes, alight with argument and energy.

And so, with the discovery of these kinds of shared attitudes and shared passions, they soon discovered they liked the way their respective minds, behind the looks (to which they were initially attracted), turned over.

Now, he is lounging back on the lawn, idly eyeing the two-storey manor house in front of him while chatting about the local butcher and what a slippery customer he is. Didn't she know? And he is about to continue when they hear voices coming from the direction from which they too had entered the estate. Without a word, both tacitly acknowledge that these voices may very well be those of the property owners, inconveniently come back just in time to spring them trespassing. They gather their things and scramble behind a line of thick bushes and low trees that look down upon the rose garden, but in which they will be safely hidden. As they kneel on the cool earth in the dark shade of the bushes, Catherine looks up to him with her deep brown eyes smiling, noting – she will tell him later – that the Marxist in Daniel retreats fairly smartly when the landlord is on the scene.

On that same bright autumn day, a middle-aged couple set out for an early-afternoon walk. They are, at once, dressed for walking (sensible shoes) and dressed for an outing. The man, tall with a slight stoop, is especially sensible, wearing a tweed cap and light tweed trousers tucked into long socks, something like a golfer about to step out onto a fairway rather than country fields. But the top half of him, shirt, tie, light sports coat (white handkerchief tucked into the breast pocket), is attired for a more formal occasion. The woman wears one of those practical summer dresses that suit just about any situation. They give every appearance of being a couple, two people who have been together for most of their lives, who, perhaps, holiday regularly in the town and who have, for many years now, been taking regular walks through this famed countryside. It is a postcard town, surrounded by postcard fields full of postcard sheep, and, to all appearances, they are a postcard English couple. In fact, they are American. And while couples that have been together many years may indeed hold hands, they are apt not to. Even then, it is not only the fact that these two people are holding hands that is noteworthy, it is also the way they are doing it. Their grip is firm, and at times their arms swing back and forth, not like a middle-aged couple but like two young lovers. They smile at each other frequently. She carries herself with the dignified bearing of an actor about to make an entrance, and her eyes shine, not with contentment but with the sheer delight of a young woman in love – the happiness of a woman who has kept her love inside her, stoppered in a bottle, and who is only now uncorking her happiness, releasing the young woman she once was because the time is right. She is almost two women: the one young, unselfconsciously releasing her happiness; the other mature, watching it all unfold. Together they experience everything twice over.

If they are any kind of couple, they are a mature couple giving themselves licence to be young. For they first met in what must now seem to them like another world altogether, and is: Boston before the war, when she was eighteen (she is now forty-three) and he was twenty. She is Emily Hale, Miss Hale to the drama students she has left behind at a Californian girls school. She is a frustrated actor and always yearned for the theatre but having been born into Boston aristocracy she was forbidden by her guardians (her aunt and uncle, with whom she is staying in the town) to step on to the stage as a professional.

Miss Hale has left the job that she loves and her friends to be with this man whom she calls Tom. Had the world outside of that tight Boston society not called to him, had he not travelled to Europe and never come back, they might well have married in their youth as everyone expected and eventually become the middle-aged couple that they now give the impression of being as they leave behind the high street in the town and head into the countryside where the ubiquitous sheep bleat and the cows wait. But, instead of living that life, this Tom of hers settled in England, married an Englishwoman, and became both unhappy and famous. When he is not being called Tom by his family and friends, he is referred to as Mr Eliot, in journals and newspapers. For this is an age in which critics of literature (and Mr Eliot is both a poet and critic) refer to their subjects as Mr So-and-So, or, occasionally, Mrs or Miss So-and-So. Mr Eliot, Mr Yeats, Mr Pound. The name that Tom – who is adjusting his cap and eyeing the fields for cattle because cattle unnerve him almost as much as humanity does – the name with which Tom presents himself to the world, the name by which he is known and read (indeed by Catherine and Daniel, who are, at this moment, discovering the disappointment of the drained pools of the estate), the name that he sends into the world with his books of verse and criticism, is T.S. Eliot. In tweeds and old cap, he is Tom. But it is in his best suit of T.S. Eliot that he is known to the world.

Emily has been living in the town throughout the summer. As soon as she arrived, Tom rushed from what society calls a 'difficult' marriage, and an even more difficult separation, to be with Emily Hale, whom he first met (and never forgot) at a Boston soiree in another life, when he had played Mr Knightley to Emily's Emma Woodhouse.

On this bright autumn day, at the suggestion of her aunt and uncle, they have embarked on the short mile or so walk to the eighteenth-century manor house of Burnt Norton. The house, they are told, is nothing special. But the rose garden, they are assured, is worth the walk. And, as the house is unoccupied, they are also assured (in the manner of a friendly wink) that they will not be disturbed. The house is not famous, and no one ever goes there.

As they enter the estate's grounds through the same gate as Catherine and Daniel had not long before, Emily Hale, who precedes Tom, pauses and notes that it would be an ideal spot from which to observe the sunset. He nods and they stroll on through the green shade, holding hands as they have for most of the walk. But as they leave this thickly wooded section of the estate and approach the open lawns, Emily rushes ahead. She turns, raises her voice as she looks up to the treetops and the sky, and loudly, theatrically, pronounces everything perfect: the day, the time, the place. She also calls back to him, demanding to know if they have everything they should. He checks his pockets and assures her that, yes, everything is here. They have all they need. Nothing has been overlooked and nothing can go wrong.

It is this exchange that Catherine and Daniel, currently lounging on the lawns in front of the house, drinking beer and chomping on cheddar sandwiches, hear. And it is this exchange (the two young people assuming it to be an exchange of the owners, not two interlopers like themselves) that prompts them to pick up their bags and bottles and take cover in a patch of thick shrubbery and low trees that look down upon the estate's rose garden.

At the same time, Emily and Tom come upon the drained circular pool. Bright sunlight (the pool is set in a small lawn, open to the sky) fills the concrete pool and they stand for a moment, speechless, transfixed by the glare. It is dazzling, but they are drawn into the intense, white reflection, struck motionless by its blinding light. Then a small cloud passes over and the pool is as drained of light as it is of water. Released from the spell, they move on, almost floating over the lawns as if in some hypnotic state until they come to two more pools a little further on. In the same trance they walk slowly, without speaking, up the path lined with roses, pass under an arch and out into the rose garden, humming pink and white in the autumn sun, which still retains the heat of summer.

In fact, neither Emily nor Tom needed to be told that the house was vacant, nor did they require the reassuring wink that they would be undisturbed. They'd already been here. They'd already discovered the rose garden the previous week, along with the pools that dazzled them then and dazzled them just now.

Today, they have come prepared. As Emily leaves the archway and walks towards a hedge-boxed bed of flowers, she takes a small pair of scissors from her dress pocket. She pauses, admiring the sun on the flowers, then selects two white roses (it is a private joke, for he affects support for the White Rose of York, which amuses both of them, for it *is* an affectation, and as much as he tries to be English, he never quite gets his 'Englishness' right) and she cuts them off the bush, looking about the property briefly before doing so.

Her 'special friend', as she calls him when talking about his letters with her 'girls' at the college or those people with whom she is not intimate enough to mention names, is standing under the arch, bewitched, it would seem, by the combined spectacle of Emily, the roses and the garden. She closes the gap between them, her eyes upon his. There is a hint of a smile on his face; his eyes are both focused on her and far away. She knows the look; he is both here and not here. He is, she knows, someone who is either continually looking back or looking forward, one of those who feel the pastness of a moment even as they are living it; who feel, at odd times, ordinary moments as if already having lived them, as if living them, and as if about to live them, all at once. He is either dogged by nostalgia or drawn into yearning for something more. She, although knowing all this, is much better at simply living the moment, in the here and now, without too much looking forward or back, or towards other worlds, other realities behind the 'appearance' of this one. Emily Hale is better at simply doing things without the eyes of Emily Hale looking on. And as she reaches for his coat lapel, he lowers his eyes and notes her nimble fingers pinning the bloom to his chest as perfectly and securely as he would dearly love to pin this moment, in all its detail, to that part of the mind where memory is contained, and which he draws upon when he picks up the pen to write. To pin these moments to a page, with such perfect ease, poetry without the poetry, that would be something. His eyes flicker, she pins the second rose to her dress, and, rising slightly on her toes, kisses him on the cheek. His face breaks into a smile and she nods.

Yes, that's it, she seems to say: just let the moment take you without too much thought, for once.

She then takes his hand, leading him through the rose garden, along the central aisle that runs in between the boxed beds of roses, pausing occasionally, pointing to this bloom and that. And when they finally come to a stop, it is at the front of the garden, underneath the windows of the unoccupied house.

He removes his cap and runs his fingers through his hair, shiny, parted down one side, with a hint of brilliantine. And as they pause, arm in arm, they look out over the garden, almost as if surveying an assembly or a congregation. The roses, in their second blooming, glow pink and white in the heavy autumn sun, witness to the couple's presence and what it is that they are about to do, for they have the appearance of two people paused on the brink of a ceremony.

With the rose pinned to his lapel, Tom inclines towards her, his figure tall and stooped, his face solemn, almost grave. She stands beside him, both facing the garden, but with their heads turned, eyes upon each other. They hold hands and it is then that he speaks, softly, slowly, almost a whisper, words that are meant for only two people to hear. It is brief, and when he is finished he raises his eyebrows slightly, in the manner of a question. Without hesitation, the moment he has finished, she nods. If, indeed, it is a question that has been asked, it has been answered with a yes.

He then lets go of her hand, puts his cap back on, reaches into his coat pocket and takes out a small rectangular container, a tin of some sort. She watches, rapt, perfectly still, as he opens it and takes out a gold ring. But it is at this moment that his head jerks up and swings about, his nose, his brow, his eyes those of an eagle as he scans the garden, not so much in search of prey as intrusion. The lightness leaves his features, his eyes are concentrated, his whole bearing one of somebody on guard. It is as though he has heard something. Was it a bird, or was it, surely not, laughter? In front of a manor house that they have been assured is unoccupied, in a garden that should be free of people, he feels disturbed. As if the occasion has been intruded upon, even mocked, the way laughter cheapens a solemn moment, and he now scans the garden with eagle eyes as if seeking out the source of hidden laughter, somewhere out there in the bushes. But the garden is silent apart from the occasional calling of birds, and the flapping of wings as they dart from one bush, one tree, to another. The eagle then relaxes, becomes Tom again, and turns back to the puzzled face of Emily, who is wondering what on earth could have caught his attention, for she heard nothing.

He lifts her left hand, as if preparing to bestow a kiss upon it, but instead slips the ring onto her third finger. She then, quite smartly (it is over in a second or two), accepts another ring that he takes from his coat pocket and puts it on his finger. He then kisses her cheek, and she his. The ceremony is done, but they linger, breathing in the moment and the warm autumn air.

When they are done, they stroll, side by side, back up the central path of the rose garden and soon kneel at the trimmed hedged border of one of the flower beds. Here he drops his cap onto the lawn, then, opening the small rectangular tin, places it on top of the low hedge. Together they unpin the roses and place them gently in the tin. Then he takes a small piece of paper from his coat pocket, and, already folded, places it in the tin with the two white roses. And finally, reluctantly, he slips the ring from his finger and puts it, too, into the tin. He snaps it shut, strolls a few feet back to the arch, picks up a stick he noticed as they entered the garden and returns to the flower bed, where he begins to dig a hole with it. The bed has been recently tended, the soil is loose, and the digging is easy. When the hole is deep enough, he buries the tin in the hole and covers it, all in an effort to make it look as though the soil has never been disturbed. But it clearly has. The only article left over from the ceremony is the ring on Emily's finger. And when she eventually returns to America, she will wear this ring in public. Friends, acquaintances, even strangers, will remark upon the ring, but not to her. And, even if they were to ask, she wouldn't tell them, for that would be to betray her special friend.

The tin is consigned to the secret earth, and they both wear the calm, peaceful expression that comes with a job well done. Then there is the sound of a motor car, loud and intrusive, coming from the driveway of the estate. Doors slam. They both look up and exchange anxious glances, then rise from where they have been kneeling and leave through the same archway by which they entered the garden, almost in the same way Catherine and Daniel fled the scene upon their arrival. They pause for a moment beneath the arch looking over the rose garden, it would seem, one last time. Satisfied, yet warily eyeing the driveway, they retrace their steps. Neither of them notices his cloth cap, lying on the lawn beside the hedge where he dropped it and which has been forgotten in their haste.

Catherine and Daniel kneel in the thick foliage beside the rose garden, hidden behind the leaves. They are perfectly still, listening to the low, muffled voices coming nearer from the path just to their left. Then a man and a woman, dressed sensibly for a walk, but also, they notice, almost formally, emerge from under the archway and Catherine knows who they are straight away. They are not the owners. They are not to be feared, but having concealed themselves in the bushes it is now impossible to reveal themselves. Besides, the couple, absorbed in their own company, give every impression that they would not welcome an intrusion.

She is the woman from America, who teaches drama at a girls school in California. She is staying with her aunt and uncle in the town, occupying one of the cottages adjoining the large house they have rented for the summer. Catherine knows this because she cleans the house and cottages every other day. Miss Hale, as Catherine calls her (although she knows perfectly well her name is Emily), has been living in the town all summer. She has even got to know her a little, for Miss Hale is a friendly woman who is very interested in everyone and everything around her. She has an enthusiasm for the town and the countryside that Catherine has warmed to, for it is not a condescending enthusiasm. It does not make Catherine feel 'quaint' as some of the holidayers in the town, from different parts of the world, do. There is also something theatrical about her, at least to Catherine, for she often talks like the drama teacher she is. Especially when referring to her 'girls' back home, almost as though she fashioned them herself, so that, wherever they went in life after their school years, whatever they did, they would always have the stamp of Miss Hale upon them. And Catherine, right from the beginning of the summer when this woman started to open up to her, could feel the pull of being one of Miss Hale's girls, of wanting to be one of Miss Hale's girls. The fun of it all, but, more importantly, that sense of being outside the march of usual female society. Of being different. Being special. Being one of Miss Hale's girls. And perhaps Miss Hale senses this, for, on the occasions that they chat (Catherine often asking about the distant wonderland of California, with its vast blue skies and sun, the likes of which she can barely imagine), Miss Hale asks what she does, and takes more interest than most people from the town in the fact that Catherine (and she is quite proud of this) will soon begin her final year at school, literature being her first love and her whole reason for studying at all; the rest, geography and maths, the things you have to get through because they make you. Miss Hale is most interested. Who does she read? Who are her favourites? Has she ever heard of so-and-so, who might be good for a young woman such as Catherine to read at this particular time of life? Yes, Miss Hale takes an interest in Catherine's studies, more than most around her. In fact, she takes an interest in Catherine's studies in such a way that Catherine is beginning to feel that she has, to some extent, been taken under Miss Hale's wing. The same wing under which she takes her girls, for Catherine has lately begun to feel, to understand, just what it might be like to be one of Miss Hale's girls. That, in just being one of her band, one automatically grows and leaves behind that fine line that separates adolescence and adulthood, being a girl and being a young woman. One is spoken to like a grown-up. One gives one's views on a variety of subjects in the company of equals. More importantly, one trusts and receives trust on the unspoken assumption that it will never (on pain of death) be betrayed. And, ultimately, one is judged fit to receive confidences. That sense of being taken under Miss Hale's wing early in the summer, the interest Miss Hale took in all she did, it struck Catherine later, might not just have come from her friendly nature but the result of curiosity, a desire to find out if this young woman was fit to receive confidences. If it was a test for which Catherine didn't even realise she was sitting, she apparently passed it. Yes, she had, it seemed, been found up to receiving what confidences Miss Hale might see fit or find necessary to bestow upon her. She had, in fact, already received one.

For it was, in just such a way, that Catherine first heard of Miss Hale's special friend. You may, she told Catherine early in her employment, you may, from time to time, see or meet a special friend of mine who comes up from London to visit. You will do me a service more valuable than work, she suggested, if you say nothing of it. And Catherine had nodded, saying nothing, both flushed with the tone of the request (one adult to another) and intrigued as to whom it could possibly be. It was all part of that world of confidences and trusts, the kind of confidence bestowed on Miss Hale's girls and the kind of trust expected of them. If, her manner clearly implied, if you were one of my girls (and if you attended my college you most certainly would be, for, you have, her manner once again clearly inferred, that something extra that all my girls have), you would know without being told the need for discretion. She doesn't use the word 'secrecy', Miss Hale. Whenever she speaks to Catherine on the subject of her special friend, she instead speaks of discretion. And care. And, on one such occasion, as if to dispel any unnecessary sense of mystery, as if to explain that this required discretion was no affectation, she spoke, in distant terms, of someone she knew, a dear friend who had made a most unfortunate match in his youth and married a very weak woman. And don't imagine that the weak don't have power, she'd said, gazing from her cottage window on to the garden below, they have enormous power. The selfishly weak will always rule the strong.

For they cling and they hold on long after they have any right to. This is the selfishness of the weak. They hold on to things long after they have any right to, just so nobody else can have them. Do you know such people, she had asked, turning her head back from the garden the way actors do on the stage. Just the way actors do when they have revealed something of their inner character and are momentarily vulnerable. Catherine shook her head and Miss Hale had smiled. Good, the smile implied. You are lucky. Let's hope it stays that way.

Without as much being said, Catherine was given to understand, very early in her employment, that such discretion was crucial, in case this woman, this weak woman, who held on to things longer than she had any right to, intruded upon their special time together. For, although she was weak, Catherine was given to understand through the urgency that Miss Hale radiated when speaking of these visits from her special friend, she was, this woman, cunning, as the weak and selfish inevitably are, and not to be under-estimated. She follows him, this woman, plagues and turns up just when he thinks he is alone. It is not an exaggeration, Miss Hale had suggested, to say there are even times when, with some justification, he can lay claim to being haunted, her friend.

'You may even know of him,' she once murmured, with the faintest of smiles, not even a smile but a hint that one was not far away, a suggestion that when Catherine was out of the room and she was alone, Miss Hale might allow herself a smile, and a vaguely satisfied one at that.

It was said in such a way that implied her friend was known to the public and that she may very well have seen his photograph in the newspaper, or perhaps not. And then, Miss Hale had dropped the matter, as if having gone too far, become too loose in her talk. For what was noteworthy to Catherine about this particular remark was that Miss Hale was not simply passing on information important in assuring that these visits were treated with discretion, but almost (and that shadow of a smile had suggested as much) in the manner of someone passing on a piece of gossip. Passing on a piece of gossip because they just can't help themselves, and, almost simultaneously, reprimanding themselves. For with that hint of a smile came the shadow of a boast. And this was what was so noteworthy about the moment: that Miss Hale was not a boastful woman and yet she had almost let one slip from her. A slip that would, in Catherine's estimation (as, indeed, it would in Miss Hale's) have been beneath the lady.

Nonetheless, when Catherine arrived one morning early in the summer to begin her tasks, she observed the tall, stooped figure of Miss Hale's friend standing by the drawing-room window of the main house, and she couldn't help but stare. She did indeed know him, and when Miss Hale saw this, Catherine noticed, once more, the caged bird of a smile fluttering beneath her control.

But she kept all this to herself (until later when she told Daniel, for she never imagined that discretion excluded him). And on each occasion, the two or three times that the matter came up in conversation with Miss Hale, Catherine nodded, making it perfectly clear that she understood everything. That discretion was guaranteed. That her loyalties could not be doubted, Miss Hale's confidences were in safe hands and her trust would be returned because Catherine was, if not in fact then at least in spirit, one of Miss Hale's girls.

And so, here they are, Miss Hale and her friend, no more than twenty feet or so away from them. Catherine and Daniel are perfectly still, two children hidden in the leaves, desperate not to be found out. It is only the second time she has seen Miss Hale's friend. He is tall, not stooped this time, his shoulders back as he stares ahead up the pathway, his stance as formal as the neatly folded white handkerchief in the breast pocket of his coat. Then, slowly, as if to unheard music, Miss Hale and her friend emerge from under the arch and stroll slowly up the central pathway of the rose garden.

They are solemn. Happy, but solemn. And it is this very solemnity that draws Catherine in. As they pass by directly in front of them, she has no fear of being discovered, for they seem to belong to another time and place altogether – a time completely outside that which Catherine and Daniel are experiencing. They are at once real and ghosts from another age. They glide by in front of her as if inhabiting another garden in another time. And, without knowing exactly why, from the bits and pieces of their history that Miss Hale has offered up in conversation from time to time, Catherine is sure that they are enacting something they never did, once upon a time, when this act was there to be performed, but which, for one reason or another, never was. And it is possibly for this reason that they seem to inhabit, as they now approach the end of the pathway at the foot of the house, another time. There is a then-and-now manner to the way they move through the garden, a grace, a solemnity that belongs to another age, and implied in it all an order of feeling that may well have gone out with the horse and buggy – an old-world couple in an age of uncertainty, with its constant newspaper talk of war and revolution and choosing sides.

They turn at the top of the path and face the garden. He removes his cap and turns to her. They hold hands. He speaks softly, words meant for two people and two people only. And the moment he is finished, his eyes raised in the manner of a question, she nods. He replaces his cap, reaches into his coat pocket and fishes out a tin of some sort, like a tobacco tin, from which he produces a small golden object. And it is then, while Catherine is absorbed in the spectacle of Miss Hale and her special friend, who now face the garden as if facing an assembly or a congregation, that she hears laughter. Low laughter, muffled laughter. But laughter nonetheless. And she is not sure at first where it is coming from, for she feels as though she has been hypnotised by the spectacle, by the day and its sleepy heat, and is only now shaking the sleep off her and returning to the here and now. Drawn back to reality by this laughter that, at first, she can't place. Then, as she snaps free of the spell the garden has cast upon her, she turns to see the curved, sneering, laughing lips of Daniel beside her. She could kill him. This is no time for laughter. Not even happy laughter, let alone the sniggering laughter of the Daniels of this world. Her heart has gone out to Miss Hale. Her heart has gone out to the Miss Hale she knows about from the scraps of personal history that have been offered up to her (how they met in a garden in Boston and parted in a garden, and are now, for all she knows, reclaiming their garden), and her heart has gone out to Miss Hale in the same way that it goes out to a paper character in a novel, a character who is travelling the winding path to what may or may not be a happy ending, depending on the whims of the novelist and the nature of the characters he has created. Please, please, her whole attitude, her whole pose suggests, let them be happy. Let nothing go wrong. They must be happy. But just as her heart went out to Miss Hale, this laughter broke out beside her, the spell was broken, and the very thing she dreaded became a possibility. For what has only just preceded his laughter is the longed-for moment when the man declares his love, the woman accepts, and happiness is theirs. While Catherine's heart was going out to Miss Hale, her special friend had taken that small golden object from the tin, which Catherine knew with absolute certainty was a ring, and was poised to place it on the finger of Miss Hale.

But as he does this, laughter erupts from Daniel, and Catherine's palm slaps hard against his mouth, sealing it and silencing him, while signalling with her eyes that she would dearly love to kill him for this. And with her hand across his mouth, she turns back to the garden path to see if the laughter has intruded upon the solemnity of the scene and notes, straight away, that Miss Hale's friend has swung round, his eyes like those of an eagle, staring right at them, and she is certain they are about to be discovered, and shame will follow when Miss Hale sees that the intrusion of sniggering laughter came from one of her girls, who was not worthy of the confidences entrusted in her, after all.

They remain silent and still, the eagle eyes of Miss Hale's friend on their part of the garden, his hand still poised in mid-air, the unwanted tension that Daniel's laughter brought to the moment still there. But soon the eyes of Miss Hale's friend return to her and smile, a smile that Catherine can see even from the distance of the bushes. As the tension breaks, his hand descends and he places the ring on her finger. He then produces a second ring from his coat pocket for her to place on his finger. She does this swiftly, and happiness is restored. With a deep sigh, Catherine drops her hand from Daniel's mouth and turns to him, shaking her head, only to see that he is still grinning. But she also sees that his eyes have a slightly glazed look. And this is when she remembers the beers they drank with their sandwiches – how he had drunk all of his bottle, for the walk was thirsty work, and then half of hers (as he always does), and she wonders if this particular local brew is not stronger than they thought. Wonders if half of this is the beer laughing along with the prankster, and ponders the possibility of some little devil having been let loose in Daniel's brain, intent on shaking things up.

Daniel knows who they are, this couple, because Catherine has told him all she knows. Catherine, actually, talks quite a lot about this Miss Hale. And she talks about her with great enthusiasm, as if she had not so much been admitted but introduced to some secret society. Or is it just that she talks about her the way a middle-class heroine in a Jane Austen novel might talk about Lady So-and-So who has condescended to take her into her confidence? He can't make up his mind, but he doesn't like the sway that this Miss Hale has over *his* Catherine. And, of course, he knows all about Miss Hale's special friend (their very language, the way they talk about each other, Miss Hale, her 'special friend' and so on, grates in itself, the way code – 'some people' and 'certain types' – in the mouths of town gossips does). He knows about this special friend. Who doesn't?

Not having heard of her friend is a bit like not having heard of Westminster Abbey. And he's got a face like the Abbey too, the way he looks down on you in those larger-than-life photographs on bookshop walls; his great nose, and great eyes. And they talk about him at Daniel's college at the university as if he *were* Westminster Abbey. Mr Eliot says this, and Mr Eliot says that (mind you, Daniel counters them by saying that Marx says this and Marx says that). And this whole Mr Eliot talk, too, like it's all some gentlemen's club, a club for which they sign themselves up (don't bother applying). No, Miss Hale's special friend is nothing more than a jumped-up snob who's got a special way with mumbo-jumbo that everyone seems to swallow whole. But what Daniel really hates is that underneath all the mumbo-jumbo, what he is really saying is wouldn't it be nice to get back to the middle ages? Wouldn't it be nice to get back a bit of order in the crumbling world, eh? Yes, underneath all that fancy, dazzling mumbo-jumbo, this special friend of Miss Hale's would dearly love to see the three-field system back, right out there, just beyond the rose garden, the empty pools and the estate grounds, out there in the fields they've just walked over, where Daniel's stride had so resolutely proclaimed to all manner of animal and vegetable life that the world belongs to everybody. And a select few, like the stuffy few in the gentlemen's club they call English Literature, watching over it all, making sure everything runs smoothly, and the muck stay in the fields where they belong, with the consolation of God just a little above their bowed heads at Evensong, or whenever it is that the muck bow their heads in thanks for all they've received. Yes, underneath all the fancy mumbo-jumbo, that's what Miss Hale's friend (and all their other like-minded friends) gets teary-eyed about having lost. And he smiles at this, tossed between the impulse to laugh again and the impulse to put a bomb underneath the whole shooting match.

But his smile fades in the face of Catherine's anger, his jaw still feeling the impact of her hand as she slapped it against his laughing mouth and silenced him. Giving him the once-over (and there's no mistaking what the look means), she returns her gaze to the scene in the rose garden in time to see Miss Hale and her special friend slowly moving back up the path through which they entered the garden, holding hands, happiness theirs. Then, halfway down the path, they stop and kneel by a bed of white roses, and it is then that he removes his cap and places it on the lawn beside the hedge and takes the small tobacco tin from his pocket, for she can see it clearly now (can even recognise, from the colouring and lettering, the brand of pipe tobacco it once contained). He removes it slowly, with a deliberation that suggests they had agreed on this before coming here, and takes the flower from his lapel, she from her dress, and together they place the roses in the tobacco tin. He then, with obvious reluctance, takes the ring from his finger and places it in the tin with the roses. Finally, he takes a small piece of folded paper and places that in the tin along with the other things. Then he snaps it shut, rises quickly, and returns with a small branch fallen on the ground nearby, and digs a hole in the rose bed, just deep enough and wide enough to take the small tobacco tin. He lowers the tin while Miss Hale watches and covers it in earth, smoothing the surface. As he does, they both suddenly look up, back towards the house (as do Catherine and Daniel) as a motor car, with loud disrespectful urgency, enters along the gravel driveway, and the sound of a motor car's doors, opening then slamming, disturbs the stillness of the day. Together they quickly level the soil so that it gives the appearance of never having been turned, then, mindful of the driveway and the possibility of prying eyes, they leave, almost hastily, pausing for a brief, reflective moment under the arch, then disappearing back along the aisle. His cap remains by the flower bed where the tin is buried, the soil by the hedge having clearly been recently dug up, despite their best efforts to hide this.

The garden belongs to Catherine and Daniel again, but it is not the same garden. And there is this motor car in the driveway. But whose? Should they stay where they are and wait? Part of Catherine would still dearly love to strangle Daniel, for his eyes still retain the disturbing look of someone with the devil let loose inside him. Be it the beer or the prankster, his capacity for the odd, crazy act is well known throughout the town. Nothing serious, nothing even wayward, just a tendency for a bit of skylarking. He's got 'go', they'll tell you in the town, this Daniel, then nod, puzzled, as if not sure just where his 'go' will take him.

And it is while Catherine is considering this and gauging the intensity of the devil in him that he suddenly kisses her, a big kiss, smack on the lips (for, despite everything, he is head over heels in love with Catherine, and she knows it), and in the manner of a mission, undertaken on her behalf, he bursts from the bushes and out into the open, now deserted, rose garden. Catherine, still crouching, half a smile on her face from the kiss, watches him, fascinated, wondering what on earth he might be up to. It's for her; she knows this. He does things for her, unexpectedly. Should she say she loves the look of someone's peaches, ripening on a tree under the summer sun, he brings one to her. And he has throughout the summer. Peaches and plums. And when she says that's theft – he'll be arrested and transported – he tells her in the manner of the teacher he will more than likely become that the peach existed in what we call a state of nature, and by investing the peach with his labour, he made it his to do what he likes with, and he chooses to give it to her. The peach was, he'd say with a grin, up for grabs.

And so she watches him, fascinated as to what he will bring back for her (roses, pink and white, she imagines) that they will pin to their shirts or simply take home as something by which to remember the day. Half dreaming, she follows his swift strides across the lawn to the flower bed, the very bed Miss Hale and her friend have just paused alongside, to the exact spot they just knelt by, and it is then that the dreamy smile drops from her face and the wonder leaves her eyes, for she knows, without doubt, what he is about to do. She rises. Bursts forth from the bushes, calling out as she does.

'No. Don't!'

But he is too quick, too agile, and she is not even sure he heard anyway. Before she can even leave the bushes behind, he plunges his hand into the soft, freshly disturbed soil, plucks the tin from the ground and holds it aloft as if it were a prize. His gift. But maybe something more than just his gift, for she knows what he thinks of Miss Hale, her special friend and everything they stand for, and she doesn't dismiss the possibility that even though he's holding it up as the prize he has won for her, this might also be Daniel's way of shaking things up a bit and getting one up on the Miss Hales and their friends of this world. Something for Catherine, yes. But something for Daniel too. As she rushes towards him, his face alight with triumph, she is ready to brain him.

Yet, even as she acknowledges this impulse, almost as soon as she stops and stands in front of him, she finds herself (eyes darting from him to his prize and back) irresistibly peering into the tin as he opens it for her. And, in so doing, in surrendering to the impulse to peer into the tin, to spy upon its contents, to satisfy her curiosity, she also acknowledges that this weakness, this impulse to peer, makes her complicit. And even as she gazes upon the freshly cut roses, the gold ring that had so briefly been upon the finger of Miss Hale's friend, and the folded piece of paper that might contain anything, she is also acknowledging that she is as bad as him. That they are jackals together. As bad as each other. But, in spite of this, even as she gazes upon the prize, she lets him have it. 'You idiot. You great, dumb village idiot!'

Sobered by her anger, and her censure, the devil bolts from his eyes. She takes one last look before telling him to close the tin. Then she attempts to collect herself. It is not, after all, a difficult situation, the calm Catherine inside her is saying. He has stolen the tin, but the garden is theirs, it is unoccupied, and they have, she reflects, all the time in the world to put the tin back in the ground where it belongs, cover it in soil, and smooth the surface for the second time, almost in as many minutes, in such a way as to suggest that the ground has not been disturbed and they are not jackals together after all.

But just as this consoling thought is passing through her mind, just as the calm Catherine inside is about to save the situation, she notices the tweed cap still sitting on the lawn beside the low hedge where it was left. And no sooner does she notice the cap than she hears their voices and the sound of their feet moving swiftly up the pathway, as yet still behind the arched wall, and she knows there will be no time to put the thing back in the ground where it belongs. And, without even trying, she and Daniel rush back to the bushes from which they have only just emerged, and conceal themselves once more, Daniel still clutching the tin firmly in his hand.

As they crouch under the leaves, they hear laughter coming towards them, as Miss Hale and her friend re-enter the rose garden under the archway. Catherine notes, the motor car presumably still in the drive (although it may have quietly left while she was letting Daniel know what she thought of his little prank), that they re-enter the garden carefree, if a little wary, look about for human presence, and deciding that the coast is clear (that the motor car merely signified some casual visitor), stroll in. Catherine is breathing deeply from the exertion of quickly retreating to the bushes and the dread of knowing what Miss Hale and her friend are about to find. As they step onto the dappled shade of the lawn, Miss Hale points to the cap. She is still pointing to it, saying, lightly, something about age and forgetfulness, as she leads him towards the forgotten object. Then all laughter stops. They stand, scarcely believing the evidence of their own eyes. He drops her hand; she turns to him as if for an explanation, as if he might know the secret cause of this travesty. For the soil has been brutally, hastily disturbed – almost as if by a dog or some wild creature from the district. A fox possibly. But in broad daylight? With people about? And as they stare at each other, silenced by what they see, the whole garden still and quiet, the silence is shattered by the loud urgent skidding of motor-car tyres in the gravel driveway at the front of the house. For two, possibly three seconds, Miss Hale, her friend, Catherine and Daniel – all four – listen with various mixtures of dread and alarm over their faces, as this motor car (which they cannot see) speeds from the driveway, stirring, they imagine, dust and stones into the air as it departs and fades into the distance of the estate's front gate. Then the garden is still again. Possessing that glowing, mid-afternoon Arcadian stillness it had a mere fifteen or twenty minutes before when Miss Hale and her friend had stood, so serenely, at the top of the garden path and exchanged rings. To all appearances still the same garden, but now utterly transformed, violated. For violation is the word that comes to Catherine while she stares at the couple she had, not so long ago, urged on to happiness, as they, in turn, stand gaping at where their intimate, shared possessions had, they assumed, been safely committed to earth, unable to fathom what manner of animal, or mad man or woman, could possibly have done this.

It is then as Miss Hale watches, helpless, that her special friend, his body folding like a summer deckchair, falls to his knees in front of his cap, in front of the hole in the earth and the glowing pink and white petals of the timeless garden, and screams out as if having been physically hit. 'I will never be free of this woman!' And as he does this, he looks in the direction of the driveway where the car has just so hastily departed, then to the hole. Catherine can't help but observe there's not only despair in this outburst but violence as well. A capacity for violence, for white-tempered, mad violence, has taken over the face and body of Miss Hale's special friend. And not just a capacity for loud violence but the kind of violent impulse that can cause people to explode and shout the most loathsome things (to 'this woman' for a start). For there is that kind of violence now in his countenance, one that, Catherine thinks, in some Jekyll-and-Hyde manner, disfigures him. She would never have thought to see such a look on the face of Miss Hale's special friend, whose public image she knows from newspapers and books, and which has always looked back at her, and all readers, with the calm, serene stare of the impersonal poet, to whom outbursts of inferior emotions are completely foreign. Human, but not like the rest of us are human. Endlessly patient. A stare that understands it all, and is above it all. And this is the image she *wants* to believe. And she is as much shocked by this violent outburst as she is by his sobs and the heaving of his body as he looks up to Miss Hale, who now kneels and takes his hands and holds them in hers, occasionally patting them and subduing him, until the violence is gone from his eyes and he is her special friend once more. When he is calmed, when they are done, Miss Hale rises, and, still holding his hands, brings him to his feet. He picks up his cap, slaps his thigh with it, and together they leave, silently, the laughter, the lightness, all gone, down the path that leads to the drained pools of the estate and the wooded section beyond that will eventually take them back to the gate she had so recently pronounced the perfect place from which to watch the sun set.

When the scene settles, for it is as though some cold, dark wind has blown in across the estate and over the rose garden, Catherine and Daniel emerge, warily, from the bushes for a second time. The screech of motor-car tyres has long disappeared, the sounds of the outburst have faded, and all is quiet again. But the sun goes behind a cloud, the shadows darken, and the storybook glow has left the garden. Or perhaps the story has changed. Catherine has the urge to shiver and feels that if she was to turn towards the house now she might catch a glimpse of a couple of ghostly figures passing across the wide windows. And this feeling that something nasty has been let loose, that something nasty might await them if they hang about too long, comes over her and doesn't leave. Nor does the impulse to shiver, as one may when walking over the ground where some distant but horrible crime was committed years, even centuries, before. Yes, it is still a storybook garden, but the story has changed and Catherine feels no desire to turn and look upon it.

It is then, in utter bafflement, that she swings around to Daniel standing beside her in the eerie stillness. 'What have you done?'

Sobered by what they have seen and heard, the

beery look gone from his eyes, he stands on the path in front of her, still clutching the tin, his eyes on the disturbed ground, as if he is just as mystified by his impulse to steal the tin as she is. 'I did it for you.'

'For me?'

'I thought you'd like it.'

'It's not a peach, Daniel. It's not a flower.'

'I thought we could have a look, and put it back. No harm.'

'Well, we can't now.'

'How was I to know they'd come back?'

'What, what, Daniel, are we going to do with it now?'

They then look back to the hole in the ground, but without speaking know it is pointless returning the tin to the earth now.

She eyes him up and down. 'You're meant to be the grown-up.'

'It was a lark. Only a lark.'

She raises her eyebrows, looks away, then back to him. 'Give it to me. Just give it to me.'

Her hand is outstretched and he places the tin in it. And quickly, like someone receiving stolen goods, she draws her hand back and whips the thing into her pocket.

Their packs over their shoulders, they leave the rose garden without looking back.

'What are you going to do with it?' he asks, as they turn at the bottom of the path, the pools that they'd come for, hoping they would be full, in front of them.

'I don't know.' Her voice is flat. The friskiness has gone out of her; the pools, the excuse to slip into their togs and get a good look at each other, to follow their ardent ways, seem, sadly, to belong to another place as well as another time. The air of the prankster has left his manner too. Catherine, seeing the sad grumpiness in his eyes, inwardly notes that the cows on the walk back to the town would be best advised to leave this intruder alone.

Shaking her head slowly, and still wondering what on earth to do with the small tobacco tin in her dress pocket, she nonetheless takes his hand and gives it a good shake as they stroll past the drained circular pool and enter the dark, thickly wooded section of the estate leading back to the gate on what already seems like another distant day, and the two of them another faintly distant couple.

A wind stirs the trees, and birds, invisible until now, lift from their perches and take to the air, full of sound and song. It is an orchestral burst of birds and music. And somewhere there is a rush of strings, jabbing, insistent, brisk, hurtling towards some emphatic, final note, signifying the end of the outing, as much as the end of a movement in a piece of music.

PART TWO

A Felt Experience
September, 1934

When Catherine arrives the next morning at the house on the high street where Miss Hale is staying, it is Miss Hale herself (not her aunt or uncle, who are presumably out and about already) who opens the door and guides her into the drawing room. She is surprised by the visit for it is not a working day for Catherine. Not that Miss Hale says any of this, but her expression shows surprise when she opens the door. But it isn't the surprise on her face that shocks Catherine, it is Miss Hale's face itself: the transformation that has taken place between yesterday and today. Her eyes are red and puffed. Her movements are nervy, even twitchy, her bearing fragile. She has either slept badly or has been crying recently. Or both. And as Miss Hale moves to the window overlooking the back garden of the property, Catherine concludes that only the combination of crying and a sleepless night could do this. For Miss Hale's face is always poised, the face of someone always in control of her circumstances, or, at least, someone who will decide her own course of action should circumstances ever become uncertain or difficult. She is that kind of woman. She has never given the impression that she is someone who could be rocked by life. But this morning the poise is gone and the control seems fragile.

Catherine, too, has spent a restless night, tossing and turning, deciding what to do with the tin, the prize that Daniel so foolishly gave her and that she would dearly love to give back, if only she could find a way.

The whole of the previous night had been given over (she can barely remember sleeping at all) to the task of finding a way. She contemplated some half-baked story about wandering to the estate and coming across a disturbed patch in the rose garden, obviously dug up by some local animal, and finding not a bone but a dirt-covered tin nearby, with this odd collection of little knick-knacks inside. Would Miss Hale like to see? And what do we make of that? Something even written on a piece of paper (which she hasn't read). Odd. And in that way Catherine could return the tin to its rightful owners and her conscience would be clear. But it was just too far-fetched. It didn't convince Catherine, and it certainly wouldn't convince Miss Hale. Besides, it would require a performance, and a very good one, just to get away with it – to even hope of getting past Miss Hale. And Catherine had never thought of herself as a performer, especially given that Miss Hale was a drama teacher who would immediately see that Catherine was acting, and very badly. Catherine, for better or worse, is incapable of lying. It would be bound to show, and she would be a nervous wreck if she ever attempted to get away with a stunt like that.

In the end the only option that rang true, was the truth itself. She would simply bite the bullet, confess, and tell Miss Hale exactly what had happened. How it had been beyond her control. How it had just been a prank. How her friend, who is good but impulsive, is known for his silly skylarking. And how no harm had been intended. She would get it all off her chest and even if she lost the friendship of Miss Hale in the process (and ceased to be one of her girls), her conscience would at least be clear and she'd be able to sleep again. And, as an offering (to show her good intentions), she'd also take with her the poems of Miss Hale's special friend, for him to sign if he pleased.

After a long and difficult night, Catherine had been resolved to get the thing over and done with as soon as possible. And with this in mind, she'd left home right after breakfast, walked up the high street, past the school at which her mother taught, and had come straight to Miss Hale before she set about whatever she had planned for the day (Catherine had not wanted to miss her and have to spend the rest of the day in a wretched state, waiting to unload her guilt). At least, she had been resolved until Miss Hale opened the door and Catherine saw her face. From the moment she looked at her, Catherine knew something was dreadfully wrong and that her timing couldn't be worse. Miss Hale was rocked, Catherine was rocked, and her resolve was shattered.

Now, Miss Hale is standing by the window, gazing out over the three-tiered garden but barely taking it in, and Catherine is frantically trying to think of a reason to justify her visit. And it is then that she remembers the book. She inwardly sighs, giving thanks for having brought it with her, for just as she remembers the book, Miss Hale turns from the view and stares at her, almost vacantly. 'What is it, Catherine?'

Just as Catherine's heart went out to her in the rose garden, so Catherine's heart goes out to her now. As much as she had willed her on to a happy ending, as much as she may have pleaded with whatever forces may have been gazing down upon the scene that nothing, nothing, go wrong, something has clearly gone wrong and Catherine is the cause of it. And all she has to do is simply reach into her pocket, reveal the tin, tell her tale, and take her punishment. That is it; that is all. Over in a minute, and surely it couldn't be as bad as she imagines. Probably a source of blessed relief for them both. Catherine could sleep again, and Miss Hale could stop crying. And so, when Miss Hale asks of her 'What is it, Catherine?', Catherine lowers her hands into both dress pockets, the one containing the small tin, the other the book, and weighs them up.

Catherine isn't sure just how long it has been since Miss Hale asked the question, but her face is becoming increasingly puzzled the more she stares at Catherine, whose answer is not forthcoming. In fact, Catherine is sure that the puzzled look on her face is slowly turning to suspicion, for the longer the silence goes on, the odder it becomes. And so, anxious at being found out, as apart from confessing, she pulls the book from her pocket and reveals it. This she says, without speaking, is the reason for her visit. And as she does, Miss Hale's face lightens, and the trace of a smile falls across it. This should uplift Catherine too, this should lighten her load. But it doesn't. She knows, even now, that this is one of those decisions (and it doesn't matter how old you are because you never forgive yourself) that will always have the power to haunt her, one of those moments when life devises a test, and we fail. This is just such a moment. And so when Miss Hale's face lightens, with the trace of a smile, she would dearly love to share in her relief, but she can't because she could have brought her so much more.

'Please,' Catherine says, holding up the book, 'could your friend sign this?'

It is a well-known edition, famous in literary circles, a standard edition that is instantly recognisable as the works of Mr Eliot. Miss Hale eyes it briefly, then looks at Catherine. 'He's gone.'

Of course. She knew as much. As soon as she saw Miss Hale's face, she said to herself, 'He's gone.'

'Oh …' and Catherine is aware of leaving a considerable pause before continuing. 'Will he be back?'

'Possibly,' Miss Hale answers vaguely, lost in sombre thoughts, then shakes herself free of them. 'He may be back,' she adds, correcting her vagueness, 'but not just yet.' As soon as Miss Hale says this, her eyes go back to the view, and her tone, her whole manner, suggests that, yes, he may possibly be back but he will not be the same. Nor will *it* be the same. Whatever the summer may have regained is now lost.

A ray of autumn sun touches Miss Hale's hair and she raises her left hand and begins to play with it, framed by the window, lit by the sun. She says nothing; the summer is ruined. Then she drops her right hand to her side, possibly a gesture of hopelessness, but almost, it seems to Catherine, as if having flung some object to the ground like an actor in a silent movie. Then she tosses Catherine a look of … reproach. Yes, that's it. There is reproach in her eyes and it is almost as if, in Catherine's mind, her guilt has become transparent, and Miss Hale now knows that Catherine's visit is a sham and that she is, in some way, the cause of all this. Even if she doesn't know how, the shifty, guilty look in Catherine's eyes (which Catherine is sure is there for Miss Hale to see – a window on to her duplicitous soul) tells Miss Hale that Catherine is at the bottom of all this and she was a fool to even consider her worthy enough to be one of her girls. But the accusation in Miss Hale's eyes fades, and she observes Catherine once more, with curiosity this time. 'You like the poems?'

'I love the poems.'

Here Miss Hale pauses again, her hands once more in her hair, and ponders the girl in front of her, as if to say, you are lucky, my dear, you are most fortunate that it is only the poems you love. 'Why?'

This is a different Miss Hale. The question is almost blunt. And Miss Hale is not a blunt person. But she has just asked a question with the sudden bluntness that people use when they are really saying, I liked you once but I'm really not sure I like you any more, so let's drop the niceties. And while Catherine is contemplating this, she is also formulating an answer to the question, so bluntly put. 'Because when I read them I feel I understand them, and nobody else does. Silly, of course.'

Miss Hale ignores the concession to silliness. 'You feel that they are *your* poems?'

'Yes.'

'Written for you?'

'Not exactly.'

'Has anybody ever written a poem for you?'

'No.'

'Not even your young friend?' and here Miss Hale smiles and inclines her head slightly as if to say, yes, I have noticed. I have seen you about the town with your friend. I miss nothing.

'No, he brings me things.'

'How nice,' and it is said without irony, implying that the times she has seen them about the town she has liked what she has seen.

'Yes, it is.'

'What things?'

'Fruit. Flowers. Little things.' And here Catherine once more fingers the tin in her dress pocket and looks anywhere but into Miss Hale's eyes.

She does not reply, but there is a softening of Miss Hale's features, as if, inwardly, she is deciding that she likes this girl, this young woman, this Catherine, after all. And in a moment of clarity, Catherine is telling herself that Miss Hale never suspected her of anything. That was just Catherine's guilt. Miss Hale has simply been rocked by certain difficult events, that is all, and she is currently not herself. And Catherine should not take it personally. All the same, she is beginning to see that there are undiscovered sides to Miss Hale, and that there could be a certain hardness, even calculation, beneath all the grace and the poise and the manners if you ever fell out of favour. An ability to turn, and quite suddenly, should she feel the need to.

It is while Catherine is contemplating all of this that Miss Hale scrutinises her as she would one of her girls. 'How old are you, Catherine?'

'Eighteen.'

'Ah,' and she nods knowingly at the garden. 'Eighteen.'

It is said with sadness, with tenderness, and with the faint suggestion, Catherine imagines, that just as her heart had gone out to Miss Hale in the rose garden the day before, Miss Hale's heart is now going out to her and whatever fate may have in store for her.

'I remember eighteen. I see it so clearly, even now. I know to the young it must seem impossible that someone of my years could ever have been eighteen, but I see it clearly.'

Catherine is on the verge of saying no, she doesn't think that at all, but Miss Hale offers only the slightest pause before going on – either out of the desire not to have her thoughts broken or the fear of Catherine's silence. 'I'm standing in a garden. There are flowers in my arms.' Miss Hale's eyes are fixed on the garden in front of her and her voice becomes dreamy, even distant, not so much, it seems to Catherine, in the way that people go when they're slipping back into the past, but in the manner of an actor playing somebody slipping irresistibly back into the past. Someone playing a role. What is more, someone used to playing the role, as though that's all they've got to hang on to now, like people who make up the past in a way it never was but who play the role so often they eventually come to believe it is true.

Miss Hale goes on to paint a vivid scene for Catherine. A garden, a long-ago garden. Miss Hale, eighteen, with flowers in her arms. And a young man, a handsome young man of whom great things are expected, is standing beside her. They have the garden to themselves. A party is in progress in the drawing room of the house behind them. Figures pass by the windows, laughter erupts. But the garden is still. Without turning from the view, Miss Hale tells Catherine that she remembers only happiness at this particular moment, which is why she remembers the moment so clearly. It is the thrill of pure happiness she remembers, the kind of happiness that you can only have when you are eighteen, with everything in front of you and no conceivable impediments to your happy progress. She can, she says, remember no other moment of such pure happiness and concludes that she was never so happy in the whole of her life, before or after, as she was at that particular moment in that long-ago garden when she stood at the foot of the garden steps, with flowers in her arms, and the young man of whom great things were expected standing beside her. Then the young man, who until that moment had remained silent, who had been content to gaze upon her, spoke, and a shadow fell across the autumn garden (as it now conveniently did on the garden outside), across her happiness, and across her eighteen-year-old heart. He was going away, he told her. For a year, possibly more. He was going away to Europe to study. Either she did not know of this or she had pushed the knowledge of his departure aside. She reacted with surprise, no, with shock. And it was then, she tells Catherine, as the shadow of his going away fell across her happiness, that, in the manner of a reflex, she threw the flowers to the ground and watched as they came to rest, motionless, on the lawn. And even now, Catherine watches as her arms fly out, flinging the phantom flowers to the ground all over again. At the same time, Miss Hale turns from the view and stares directly at Catherine, her eyes filled with … what? Catherine meets the look, a momentary one, but in that moment concludes that it is resentment that has filled Miss Hale's eyes. A resentment that does not seem to be directed against any particular person, but a general resentment that such pure happiness could disappear so quickly, so easily, and that the world could let her down so casually.

And, as if the flowers really were at her feet, as if she were turning away, not just from Catherine but from the young man of whom great things were expected in that long-ago garden of her nineteenth year, Miss Hale returns to the view, lost to the world, immersed in the combination of pleasure and pain that make the memory, even now, so immediate and clear. 'Can we ever have them back, Catherine? Those years, those gardens and the door we *would* have opened. Can we ever have it back or are we just plain childish and silly to try?'

'I don't know.'

'No, how can you? You've got it all in front of you, haven't you? Eighteen, a handsome young man. Why should you even think about losing it?'

'But I do.'

'You do?'

'Yes.'

'But why?'

'He's leaving at the end of the month.'

'Who is?' Miss Hale's eyes are alert, back in the present, in the here and now, as if her dreamy indulgences have caused her to miss something of vital significance.

'Daniel,' says Catherine, as if to say who else could we be talking about.

'Is that his name? The name of your young man.'

'Yes.'

'Where is he going?'

'To Paris. To study.'

'Oh.'

And at this point, as the two women stare at each other in silence, Catherine experiences, once again, the feeling she had just a little while before, that the heart of Miss Hale is now going out to her because Catherine is one of her girls, after all. And just as Catherine had willed Miss Hale on to happiness in the rose garden of Burnt Norton, demanding of the world and the forces that determine our fates that nothing must go wrong, she now feels certain Miss Hale is demanding of the fates exactly the same for her.

And it was also then that Catherine's fingers stroked the tobacco tin in her dress pocket, and then that she knew, beyond doubt, that she could never reveal the tin to Miss Hale. For, and she was sure of this, she was one of Miss Hale's girls now, and she would have to live with her treachery as best she could. Miss Hale had lifted her wing and taken her under it, and Catherine had the distinct feeling of handing over some part of herself, of delivering some part of herself, or whatever it was that may remain of the autumn, into the care and the judgment of Miss Hale.

It would, Miss Hale suggests, be best for Catherine to simply keep the book, so that it is ready to hand when her friend returns. His visits, she cautions, may well prove to be more erratic now and she would not want to deprive Catherine of the poems that she understands so well, and that nobody else does.

Miss Hale holds the book on the flat palm of one hand, almost weighing it – not only the volume itself, but weighing up the burdens of the author, those who share, add to or ease those burdens, and the life that had to be lived in order to produce the words.

He will, she says, come back when he feels he can. When the time is right. And it is as she hands back the book and as Catherine pockets it that Miss Hale reminds Catherine of the consequences of making a bad marriage. Her friend, she explains again, made just such a marriage. And this woman, this weak, selfish woman, is proving impossible to leave. Like all weak and selfish people, she clings to the things she has no right to cling to any more and turns everything into a nightmare. She hounds him at his work (the poor man has to escape through the back door), she follows him and appears when he least expects (she bobbed up at a book signing one day). And, most recently, she shattered the most private and beautiful of ceremonies (and although Miss Hale makes no specific mention of a place and time, Catherine knows exactly what she is talking about, and wishes once again that she could summon the courage to just reach into her dress pocket and produce the tin, and say,

'Here, here it is. It is not what you think,' but she doesn't). And this, Miss Hale says, this desecration of a deeply private moment, is the reason he has gone. Because, she goes on, until now they had this place to come to, and it was all theirs, away from all the cares of the past and the all-too-immediate present. A place both secret and private. But like one of Mr Blake's worms, she, this woman, found it out. Oh, she may not know exactly where they are, but she knows the general vicinity. Thank heavens, Miss Hale adds, it's a popular region. And there is a glint in her eyes, a hint that this is precisely why it was chosen for their rendezvous in the first place. Then her gaze rises to the ceiling, as if to suggest that Catherine can't possibly imagine the effect of all this.

'Have you ever heard of the Furies?' she asks, and Catherine shakes her head. 'No, no, why should you?'

The Furies, she goes on, also expressing the hope that Catherine never meets them, are avenging goddesses who won't let you be. They are, she says, the nightmare that follows you about in broad daylight. Of course, Catherine has heard of the Furies but had simply never considered the possibility that Miss Hale might be referring to them;

she finds it inconceivable that anybody could seriously imagine themselves being followed by gods out of a Greek tragedy. That is just plain silly. But Miss Hale goes on, treating the whole idea as completely plausible, and Catherine is considering the possibility that such people might exist – as might the ghostly gods that follow them in broad daylight, making oohing sounds in the ears of those they pursue. No, no. Impossible. The people who believe in the gods enough to make them real might exist, but the gods don't.

'The poor man,' Miss Hale continues. 'He feels as though all he's got to do, anywhere, anytime, is turn, and they'll be there. And so he spends his days ignoring them, in the hope that if he ignores them long enough they'll go away. But they don't. And, of course, it's not *them*, is it?' she adds with sudden vehemence. 'It's *her*!'

She sinks onto a chair beside the window, exhausted by the whole scene, and the final utterance that seems to have wrung the last of her energy from her. That, and the bad night to which her eyes bear testimony.

After a long pause, in which she seems to have completely forgotten all about Catherine, she turns and smiles, nodding, acknowledging that, in this young woman, she has found a patch of fresh air in a tired, stale world. 'He, my friend, assures me that he will return when he feels he can. He is very busy. But when he returns, he will, of course, sign your book. I will see to that.' She smiles at Catherine as if to say that is that. Their conversation is now concluded.

Catherine nods back, then turns to the door as Miss Hale rises from the chair to let her out. But as much as she is finished with the conversation, Miss Hale lingers in the doorway, looking this breath of fresh air up and down, and smiles. 'Eighteen. I remember eighteen.'

Out in the high street, following the curve of the road down to the marketplace, Catherine reaches into her dress pocket. The tin is there; of course it is. She had gone to give it back, to tell Miss Hale that it was all a silly prank that went wrong, but failed in her errand. Now they're imagining Furies, and wicked women who won't let things go are at the bottom of all this, when all the time it was a silly prank gone wrong. All she had to do was just give it back and unburden herself – and all of them – but she didn't. And although she could feel the weight of the thing in her pocket, they were all weighed down by it now. And the moment that undid them won't go. She's convinced herself that the sensation of carrying around some sort of weight from these days won't ever go now, and she will always be carrying it around with her. There was no giving it back, she'd missed her chance. Now she was a fake, and she knew it. One of Miss Hale's girls, but also the cause of Miss Hale's sleeplessness and tears.

She stops, gripped with the impulse to throw the thing away, to walk down to the stream that flows near the town and throw it in. But what good would that do? The tin would be gone, but its weight would remain. And as she grips the tin and gives it a shake, she hears, faintly, a small metal object rattling around inside.

She'd also wanted to tell Miss Hale that eighteen wasn't so wonderful, anyway. That she'd been eighteen for most of the year and she'd never felt so alone. Until she met Daniel this summer, and, for the first time in her life, felt that there really was someone for her after all. And although she knew he was going away and may very well come back to her as he insisted he would because she was beautiful and he was head over heels in love, he might not either (her mother had married a man who was head over heels in love with her and he'd never come back). But, for the moment, there really was someone out there for her, and that had made all the difference to the summer. But it had nothing to do with being eighteen, and everything to do with meeting Daniel.

A little while later she is sitting on a bench by the stream that runs through the town at the back of the high street, the sounds of sheep all around, the field in front of her glowing a deep autumn yellow. Still dwelling on the conversation with Miss Hale, she reaches into her pocket for the book (for no particular reason that she is aware of) and begins flicking through it. Her eyes are skipping over the pages, barely taking in the writing, when she stops. She stops because she has come to a poem about a crying girl, which she has read before but not closely. A girl, a young woman, is standing in a garden. There are flowers in her arms, which she flings to the ground, then looks back at somebody, somebody who is in the garden with her, with resentment in her eyes. It is, Catherine quickly realises, a farewell scene, but one that is almost acted, like a silent movie.

Catherine looks up from the book and stares out across the field. Had she previously read the poem more closely than she thought? Had she taken its images in more than she thought? And when she had stood listening to Miss Hale this morning, had she arranged the scene in her mind and imposed the poem upon her? Or, had Miss Hale absorbed the poem so much that, in time, she felt that this was the way it happened, this was, in fact, the way her friend had left all those years before, and, as a consequence, did she become the crying girl? And so, this morning, did she play the scene like that, knowing that Catherine would be familiar with the poem, and see, straight away, that she, Miss Hale, was the girl who cried, flung flowers and looked up with resentment in her eyes? All so that Catherine would understand that it was she, Miss Hale, who was the inspiration for so many of the poems that Catherine loved, and which she felt that she understood and nobody else did? That it was Miss Hale who was always in the lines or written in between them? Always there, in some shadowy way or another. But always a shadow.

The bleating of the sheep, the stream, the yellow glow of the field all disappeared and dissolved. All she could see was the artfully framed picture of Miss Hale that morning as she stood at the window, and she was asking herself if shadows ever tired of being shadows. Do shadows long for substance? Do muses, consigned to background silence, ever grow tired of their silence? And is this what Miss Hale was doing, stepping out from the shadows? You are familiar with the poem, she might have been saying, now you are privileged to learn where it came from. But, as much as Catherine finds this intriguing to contemplate, there is also something disappointing in this. For it reminds her of that flicker of a smile she detected on Miss Hale's face when she told Catherine that she may know her special friend (in the way that ordinary people know the famous). There was a hint of … what? Yes, a hint of gossip about the whole episode that was beneath the lady, but which the lady couldn't resist revealing, all the same.

It is while she is turning all of this over that she remembers the uneasy feeling she had at the time – that Miss Hale was acting. That Miss Hale was a drama teacher. And that she was putting on a performance for both Catherine and for herself. And, in so doing, the shadow stepped out of the shadows and assumed solidity; the background muse grew tired of her silence and found her voice. Her special friend may have departed (and she may very well be losing him – for the second time) but she at least had this: the knowledge that she had made it all possible. And with that knowledge came the role that she was now playing, a role that one could so easily step into and live for the rest of one's life because that's all one is left with. And so when the world closes in, when things go wrong and her dream of retrieving something of the past looks set to come crashing down around her, she becomes not just Miss Hale but the crying girl herself. It not only gives her a place to go, and a time when anything is still possible, but … a what? A consolation? That even if her dream comes crashing down, she will always be the crying girl. She will always have that to show for it all. But only if somebody knows. For, as surely as the poem doesn't exist until somebody has read it, neither does the muse.

Then, as Catherine closes the book, another thought occurs to her. Had Miss Hale, quite simply, always been an actor? Had she played the scene like a melodrama the first time in that long-ago Boston garden, and had her special friend seen the actor in her and simply written down what he saw? A beautiful young woman living in the dream world of the stage that her guardians forbade her from entering. And because of that, did she then pour all her theatrical longings (and her storybook love) into the theatre of life itself? Did he see this? And did he catch sight of her in a way that she never could because he was standing beside her watching the performance and she was in the thick of it?

Now, as she rises from the bench, Catherine takes with her not only the weight that comes with that small metal tin in her pocket but also the puzzling feeling that she has entered an odd story, one of those little drawing-room plays that people in books put on from time to time to amuse themselves on a drizzly day, or to pass the time on a dull afternoon.

'I couldn't do it. I just couldn't.'

Catherine and Daniel are walking across open country outside the town. It is late in the afternoon, the shadows of trees lengthening over the fields. They have set out with no particular destination in mind, and when she suggests they head for a small town nearby, she knows it is too late even as she suggests it and when Daniel shakes his head she agrees. Besides, they have not come out here to walk to some designated place, but simply to be alone.

'He's left – her special friend. She's been crying all night, and they're blaming it all on this wicked woman he married, who apparently won't let him be. It's ridiculous! All I had to do was just stand there and set the record straight. But I couldn't.' At this point she looks across at Daniel as if she could strangle him all over again for getting her into this mess.

'I'm sorry,' he says, catching the look in her eyes.

Catherine doesn't seem to hear or notice. She continues as if he has not spoken. 'She tells me things in this funny way. Rather quaint. She turns it all into a little play. Honestly, I feel as if I've walked into a Henry James novel, and she's desperately trying to tell me something, but she can't just come out and say it. Today she played a scene for me.' She eyes

Daniel, to emphasise the point. 'I mean it, she *played* a scene. Does she know she's doing it?'

Daniel shrugs his shoulders. He doesn't know, the shrug says. 'A scene? Of what?'

'Something that happened when she was young, and I kept on thinking, this is familiar. But how?' Catherine then stops and looks around, indicating they've probably walked long enough. 'Later, I was flicking through my book of his poems, and there it was. The whole scene. Everything perfect. The look, the flinging of the flowers, the farewell. It was all there.'

'Is she touched?'

'No, she's just sad, I think. And I could have made her happy. But I couldn't do it. I just couldn't. In the end I just stood there and listened to it all with this bloody tin in my pocket. And don't say sorry again or I'll brain you.' But she kisses him instead. Out here in the fields, with only the sheep looking on, they are free to do as they wish – provided no yokel comes strolling by. As much as she may have had the impulse to brain Daniel, she succumbed to the impulse to make love instead. To 'make love', she well knows, is to kiss, to embrace – to be ardent. And when Catherine thinks of making love, she thinks of these things. But she also thinks about what comes after all the kissing and embracing. The undressing, the nakedness. Not so much a mystery as unknown. Hard to picture. Oh, she can picture certain things, whole scenes. But they are just pictures. Imaginings. She is sure that whatever really happens will be something quite different. Something for which she is unprepared and will always be unprepared unless she plunges. And so she is frightened of whatever it might prove to be, but wants it as well. With Daniel. For Daniel has come along. And with Daniel coming along has come a picture of what follows after the kissing. What some books call 'intimacy'. What others call 'going to bed'. If you have a convenient bed to go to. Some of the young girls from the town have made their way out to these fields on summer and autumn nights, and already done it with other young men of the town. A few have even got themselves in the family way. But only a few, for as much as she's been warned off 'going too far' (and that is another way of putting it) by the school mistresses because it would make you a 'fallen' woman and get you pregnant, her observations of couples and marriages in the towns she's lived in have taught her that it is actually rather difficult to get pregnant.

During the summer with Daniel, Catherine has reached a point where she has tired of simply thinking about all this, she wants to *know* it, this mystery dance that everybody knows the steps to and that she doesn't. Not yet. Most of all, she's met the boy she wants to dance with. Or, rather, she's met the boy, and, well, now feels that the inevitable should inevitably follow. She smiles briefly to herself because she imagines that Daniel would like that line (he's the sort that likes lines), even though she stole it from a favourite book by Mr Somerset Maugham. But she doesn't tell him because she's dwelling on the summer and the happy coincidence of Catherine and Daniel that has transformed it. And she has more than a sneaking feeling that all the talk from her school mistresses about pain and hardship and duty is just the talk of middle-aged spinsters who've never actually done it, never would, and who now console themselves with the belief that they are better off without it.

So, when Catherine makes love to Daniel, when she kisses him and holds him, as she does now (instead of braining him), she feels pleasure. She likes to receive pleasure and she likes to give it. Her nature is ardent. And as she kisses Daniel, she remembers again that 'ardent' is their word.

But they have a problem: nowhere to go. The local girls may be happy to give themselves up to a roll in the country fields with their young men but Catherine isn't. For her, there is nothing romantic about rolling around in a country paddock with the grass and the dirt and the sheep bleating. You went there because you had nowhere else to go, and, if you weren't careful, you came back with grass stains all over your dress telling everybody in the town or within eyeshot exactly what you'd been up to. No, *they* were 'going to bed'. And she's communicated this to Daniel, who understands perfectly, because, for all the crazy little pranks he gets up to, Daniel is head over heels in love with Catherine, and, for all his professed belief in the objective forces of History, he has precisely the kind of subjective outlook, the kind of sensitive nature, that would make him a complete disaster in a revolution. He (as does she) has no time for all that guff in the novels of the infamous Mr Lawrence, where that combination of earth, dirt and sex becomes the gateway to some long-lost organic society. No, it was so serious you couldn't take it seriously – that world in which characters knew each other with the fullness of 'dark knowledge' as they rolled around in country fields exchanging all their vital sensual reality and whatnot. Catherine and Daniel, in fact, have had many amusing conversations in the language the two of them call Lawrence-*sprechen*. The infamous Mr Lawrence may have been worshipped back at university, but Daniel just had to laugh. And so he agrees with Catherine. *They* are 'going to bed'. But where? Friends' places? His friends were all back in Cambridge. And he didn't have a room at university any more. He was leaving; he'd finished his degree. He'd really only come back to the town to say goodbye to his father – the town itself did not mean a great deal to him. He'd only been vaguely aware of Catherine. That she was new, that her mother was a school teacher. He hadn't counted on this – on their spending the whole summer together and now the beginning of autumn. On, well, falling in love. But he has, and soon enough he'll be off. It was all planned. All organised. Tickets. Places to stay, people to meet. The whole venture has acquired an inevitability that can't be avoided. But he's fallen in love, and now it is complex. And time is dwindling.

And so as their mouths unglue and they look about, they are still confronted with the same problem. The problem that has plagued them all through the summer and into the autumn. The problem still unresolved, like a question left hanging in the air as they talk and wander back to town.

Later, the sun sinking over the town, Emily Hale watches from a market stall as this Catherine (to whom she has become attached and whom she trusts, as she would one of her girls) kisses, briefly, her young man in the street. It is a brief kiss but filled with implication – that they would be more than happy to linger over each other in this way but not in the plain view of the street, with its market-day stalls. The restraint on the part of these two young lovers adds, she notes, poignancy to the brevity of the kiss, giving it a force and power that almost makes the kiss, to the observer, a felt experience. A 'felt experience'? This phrase occurs to Emily Hale because Catherine has recently used it in her presence. And it seems to have stuck the way some phrases do, for it comes back to her now as she watches the young lovers, while also congratulating herself on being 'up with' the latest terms.

If she were to tell Catherine this (and Catherine is oblivious to her presence, has no awareness of being observed at all – not by anybody who *matters* that is), one part of her would smile. For it is a fashionable phrase that the critics Catherine reads use now when they are talking about poetry – that the right words, used in precisely the right way by someone gifted in the use of words, provide the reader with a 'felt experience'. It is also the test of great writing – if it is 'felt' or not. Catherine is happy with the phrase for she is sure she knows what it means and that good writing has exactly that effect on her: she feels as if she is there, in a story, with all these characters she cares so much about. And so, when a character bites into a ripe peach, one feels the skin break and tastes the juices, and with this feeling comes a hearty regard for the power of words. Catherine is continually told by those who write about poetry that words aren't what they used to be. Once upon a time, the things people did and felt and the words they used to describe it were all one. Words had natural power. And mattered. Not in the modern world. But a 'felt experience' brings back the glory days of literature when words did matter, and with that brings back the promise that words might just matter again someday – someday soon, when people will tuck into a book as they tuck into a pie. Daniel calls it waffle because as much as he is one of these sensitive types who would be completely lost in a revolution, he not so much smells a rat as a dusty gentlemen's club where everybody sits around sniffing all this 'felt experience' like they would a vintage port, while the 'felt' reality of the actual world goes completely unnoticed outside in the mines and factories where people are ground daily into early death.

Nonetheless, when Emily Hale, from the safe distance of a market stall, watches the lips of the two young lovers reluctantly part, it is a felt experience. With the experience, comes a familiar yearning. And, once more, her heart goes out to this eighteen-year-old Catherine, to whom she has become attached, whom she has taken under her wing, a protectiveness that now has added urgency because she knows that the young man, whose lips Catherine would dearly love to taste again if they were not in plain view of the street, is leaving soon. Leaving for foreign parts, just as a young man once left her.

They are a young couple who haven't yet discovered, because they are too young, that when young lovers part, even ardent young lovers, they do so forever. Her heart goes out to them, but she is also aware it is not only for the eighteen-year-old Catherine and her young man that her heart goes out.

At first Catherine isn't sure what it is that has caught her mother's attention, for her mother has, from time to time, looked up from the armchair where she is preparing her lessons and glanced at her daughter with puzzled curiosity. But it is almost furtive, and each time Catherine catches her glance, her mother quickly looks down again. The next time she looks up Catherine is quick enough to follow her mother's eye and sees she is looking at her dress – at her knee, to be precise. And at first this is a mystery to Catherine, until she sees it, the thing that has caught her mother's attention – a grass stain.

Catherine's impulse is to cover the spot with her hand or the newspaper she is reading, but concludes that there is no point concealing it now. It has been spotted and conclusions are being drawn. Presumably disturbing ones. Now, it is Catherine's turn to study her mother, with her eyes on the notes in front of her, her face hidden under her dark, springy curls, almost wiry, the complete opposite of Catherine's hair. Catherine's deep brown eyes come from her mother, but her hair, fine and straight, comes from her father. Her mother taps lightly on the notes with the pencil she is holding, as she always does when thinking or pretending that she is. She hasn't looked up since Catherine noticed the grass stain (for the first time) because, Catherine concludes, she knows her daughter is on to her. She now knows what her mother has been furtively staring at, and her mother is now scrupulously avoiding staring. Which, of course, only draws attention to the fact that she was staring. When two people have lived closely together over many years, Catherine thinks, they learn to read each other's movements and gestures. And just as Catherine is sure her mother knows she's on to her, she is also sure that she is drawing disturbing conclusions about the stain on her dress. Her mother is thirty-eight, and to Catherine's knowledge has only ever had anything to do with one man – Catherine's father. And although he bolted on her, she never passed on to Catherine any of the anger that she must have felt. She has never been warned off men, never been told that they are all shiftless and untrustworthy and only ever want one thing, although, in the circumstances, her mother would have been perfectly entitled to. No, Catherine's mother, a school teacher in the town, has always seemed remarkably composed about the whole affair. Who knows, she might have been glad to be shot of him. She has said as much on a couple of occasions, how she's watched bad marriages stumble from bad to worse through the years, putting on a brave face to the world and doing nobody any good, and how she was possibly lucky to get it all out of the way and over and done with years before. And everybody, especially Catherine, better off for her father having bolted because he would have been a dead weight and bloody pest anyway. And the only thing you could rely on, of course, was his *un*reliability. Still, nobody likes to be left, and the two of them must, at some time, have had something that's worth getting a bit teary about, her mother and this father of hers whom she's visited back in Manchester from time to time, as you would an uncle. So Catherine has never felt that the hurt or whatever damage may have been done has been passed on to her. And this is something for which she is now grateful. She has, at school and in the towns they've lived in, seen the damage done in damaged homes passed on from parents to children, as if it were only right and proper that they share the damage as they would the household jobs, one big happy damaged family. But not her mother. In fact, the older she gets (the grey is emerging where her hair parts in the middle, but she is free of lines around the eyes and mouth, Catherine is pleased to note), the more she admires her mother for containing the effects of the whole business, and for always having given Catherine, much more than other girls she has known, a certain independence. But it has always been understood as an independence that comes with responsibility for one's actions. This, the fact that she is an only child and that there has been no father in the house, has always made Catherine seem (to others as much as her mother) like those children who grow up young, more mature than their years, capable of observations and a sort of wisdom that they shouldn't really ought to have, except they do – and she does. But it's the assumption of responsibility that Catherine is dwelling on at the moment, and the possibility that her mother may well be drawing disturbing conclusions about the grass stain on her dress.

It is also why she doesn't tell her mother about

the tobacco tin, the estate house and the incident in the rose garden. It is precisely because she has been brought up to be independent, to decide things for herself, that she chooses to decide things for herself now. Besides, she has no desire to unload her problems onto her mother, for it has always been implicit that her mother has enough problems of her own, what with a runaway husband, a child to bring up, and a job to be done. In fact, it has long occurred to Catherine that this independent spirit that she has always been encouraged to cultivate has been not only good for the child but for the mother as well.

And so Catherine does not unload her troubles onto her mother, because she has rarely done so. What's more, her mother would simply tell her to give the thing back, and Catherine knows she can't. She would then not only have her conscience telling her to give the thing back, but her mother as well.

It is for all of these reasons that she says nothing about the incident in the rose garden, or the grass stain on her dress. This summer she has also entered the world of grown-up love, and while some girls might take their mothers with them into that world, Catherine doesn't. Daniel's reputation in the town for pranks and a general tendency to succumb to a rush of blood in a harmless sort of way has never bothered her mother. It's all part of this 'go' that the town (and Catherine's mother) thinks he possesses. He has, after all, gone to Cambridge – something no one else in the town has ever done (and which Catherine, too, hopes to do in a year, although she doesn't know what to do afterwards, for she has watched her mother over the years and has no intention of ever teaching). And although the town, like Catherine's mother, has sometimes wondered where Daniel's 'go' will take him, the general consensus has been that the wayward is more than balanced by the sensible. So, it is not as though her mother would be dwelling on the image of her daughter tumbling in the hay with some yokel, getting herself in the family way and ruining her life.

No, that is not Catherine's way. No tumble in a sheep paddock for her. Poets might get all dreamy eyed about fields and wenches and a jolly bit of summer sport, but Catherine's going to have a room – a room that will forever after (should they stay together or not) become their room, the place to which their ardent ways finally led them. For, if Catherine has any poet in mind at all, it is Mr Donne and that room he shares with his 'thou' that becomes an everywhere. She, too, wants such a room, but where?

Catherine's mother is back to her lesson preparations, the quick, dark eyes that she passed on to her daughter concentrating on the handwritten notes of her lesson plans for the coming school term. Catherine is back to her newspaper, with its talk of Europe and the sniff of war. Herr Hitler, she muses, wants the whole of the Rhineland – all Catherine wants is a room. Surely that isn't too much to ask of the world.

For what seems to Daniel to be at least the hundredth time, he is explaining to his father just why he is going to Europe when he really ought to be going to work. Scooting off to France, his father calls it. And why? There are schools here he could be teaching at, earning his keep. Life isn't one big stunt, or doesn't he know that? His father's hair falls across his forehead as he glances up, his lean frame hunched over the table and a look in his eyes of both irritation and pride as he gazes upon his son. Yes,

Daniel does know that. But as much as he has explained that his field of study is the French Revolution and that the logical place to go to further his studies is France (not to mention the fact that he has no desire to teach in schools anyway), he knows this isn't the full picture.

The fact is that Daniel, as much as having fallen in love with Catherine, has also fallen in love with new ideas. And Europe. The two have become intertwined. Unlike so many of those around him at university who look with suspicion and distrust on any thinking that comes out of Europe (with all its fancy notions and equally fancy talk), Daniel likes many of these thinkers. He feels, and has felt for some time, like someone who is groping towards a way of looking at History and Literature and the world around him that doesn't yet exist; a way of looking at the world that doesn't ignore the everyday life of ordinary people and all the things that they do that occupy their time, but that don't count as something serious or worthy enough of study. Not, at least, to the likes of Miss Hale and her friend. It might come as a surprise to his father or Catherine's mother or the butcher down the road that the films they watch in the towns nearby or in the town hall on weekends, and which give them a few hours of escape, pleasure or fun, might one day be worthy of serious attention. But it would not surprise Daniel. And he has got it into his head that this thing he feels he is groping towards is over *there* somewhere. Europe. Not *here*. That whatever lies scrambled in his brain will become unscrambled there. But he keeps it quiet. And so, if he doesn't mention this to his father, it is not that he is being deliberately deceitful (although Daniel has done some crazy things, he has never lied to his father), it is simply that he doesn't yet understand this impulse to go there. He just knows he has to. He has not given his father the full picture because he can't.

So where does this impulse to leave come from? The desire for fun? Adventure? Yes, but of a particular kind. If you like, the *serious* fun of grand ideas. And it is not because ideas of moment and immediacy might shake things up and change the world to greater or lesser degrees. It is the sheer excitement of ideas themselves. The thrill of understanding them. Especially new ideas. New ideas take you somewhere, and you don't need mountaineering boots to get there. Just a room and books and a place that shares your excitement.

It was the informal talks of a German scholar visiting the university (whose talks seemed to have come along at just the right time, as these things so often do) that caught his interest. When the German talked (and again Daniel hadn't let on to his fellow students that he liked what he heard – because they didn't), he caught glimpses of new ways of thinking, exciting ones – and so, for this reason, Daniel has been seized by the idea of Europe and what they're thinking over there. He may call himself a Marxist, but the Marxism of fellow students, who see literature only in terms of serving a cause, is not for Daniel. Indeed, one of those fellow students who listened to the German scholar (a Mr Adorno, who has fled the Nazis) called his ideas 'subtle'. And 'subtle' was used as a criticism, almost an insult, as if to say that this was not an age that could afford the luxury of subtle thinking. But Daniel begs to differ – and this is another reason why he would be one of the first to be lined up against a wall and shot if he were ever caught up in a revolution.

He is aware that this special friend of Miss Hale's – and it annoys him that Catherine has fallen under her spell – believes in what he calls the 'mind of Europe', for he has read the essay this idea comes from. He knows full well that Miss Hale's friend –

and he smiles to himself, acknowledging the prim, silliness of the phrase – is talking about a club of the like-minded and like-gifted (and the self-appointed, for that matter) all united by precisely the kind of exclusive idea of tradition that Daniel would dearly love to smash. And although he doesn't really know what he wants himself or what it is that is drawing him in and on, he knows that what he heard from the German scholar is different and exciting and that he is going to follow its thread and see where it leads him. It has become his passion. His other passion. Without it, he would not be the Daniel that he is. And he wants to say this to Catherine, if only he can find the right moment.

He spoke with the visiting German scholar and was given a letter of introduction to friends of his in France (many of his friends and colleagues having already fled Germany for France, England or America). Daniel has that letter, along with his tickets and his passport, in the drawer in his room at his father's house. And, with his mind half on the drawer and the exciting prospect of travel, he attempts once more to smooth his father's anxieties about his mad-cap plans, which must seem, Daniel guesses, like another of his pranks.

As his father adds up the day's takings, Daniel draws comfort from this image of his father at his work (for – and again he is at variance with many of his student friends – he is not disdainful of what they all call the *petit bourgeoisie*) and decides to let it rest for the time being. To let it rest, this whole business of trying to explain, yet again, to his father why he is passing up perfectly good opportunities for good work, when (as his father continually reminds him) so many are looking for it, for something that he can't even explain.

The fact is, for all his high-jinks, Daniel takes study seriously, as, indeed, he takes thinking seriously. Study, to Daniel, is not simply a ticket to a job (as his father would have it), something you do for a short while because it is required of you. No, study is a lifelong activity. Something he has only just begun. And, although he has told Catherine that he expects to be away for only a year, he is already beginning to suspect that it may indeed be much longer. But he can't tell her that. Much in the same way (and Daniel can't possibly know this) that Miss Hale's friend couldn't tell her, in that long-ago garden of their youth, that he might not be coming back at all. Nor can Daniel tell his father, who will simply have to understand that his son was not born for the classroom or the shop or any other of those solid work opportunities that most people in these hard days (the term 'the Great Depression' will not fall so easily from people's lips until later) would kill to have. No, that something else that he can't explain is calling him on. At the age of twenty-two he is in the thrall of exciting new ideas and has no choice but to follow them and find out where they lead him.

As his father closes the book in which he has calculated the day's takings, he rises, proposing a pot of tea before bed, and Daniel nods, vaguely noting once again the leanness of his father's frame, the sinewy hands, which, at that moment, speak of a life of simple tastes and pleasures, of someone who grew up in a world far removed from the one Daniel and his kind will inherit. His father is quietly muttering at the sink with the pot in his hands as he sometimes does (as if having forgotten that he has company, as people do when they live much of their life alone), and Daniel leaves him to his muttering.

His mind now is half on what the future may bring and wondering if he really knows why he is going, after all, and remembering, almost reliving, the touch of Catherine's lips. And suddenly he has forgotten all about those exciting new ideas, the mind of Europe and a lifetime of serious thinking because he can't conceive of anything more exciting than Catherine's kiss, and he gives himself up to the memory of her lips, and he's inwardly pronouncing himself a bloody fool for going anywhere. The Catherines of this world, he's musing, come along once in a lifetime, and she *would* have to come along just now. He never knew her, or possibly only faintly knew of her, until he came back to the town for the summer holidays, just to say a kind of goodbye to all that. But now he did know her. And a simple situation – hello, goodbye, up and off – has been complicated by the unforeseen surprise of falling in love.

The picture of Catherine and her young man stays in Emily Hale's memory. It stays with her overnight and is still there the next morning when Catherine comes to clean the house. It was a picture of young love that she observed from the distance of a market stall the previous evening, and the mixture of envy and protectiveness that it inspired has been with her since waking. And so when she greets Catherine at the door, her mind has been on this young woman for some time, although to what end she is not sure.

'Did you buy anything?' Miss Hale enquires and Catherine simply stares back at her, not sure what she means. 'At the market. I saw,' Miss Hale adds with practised casualness, 'you and your young man at the market last evening.'

'Oh,' Catherine is smiling, 'no, we didn't.'

Miss Hale retains the same casual, almost dreamy, tone of voice. 'No. You seemed very absorbed in each other.'

'Did we?'

'Yes, most decidedly.'

'You should have said hello.'

'Oh, I didn't want to disturb you.' And here Miss Hale smiles while arranging flowers in a bowl, a faint suggestion in her eyes that it would not have been an appropriate time for greetings. With the smile, Catherine blushes, for she now knows that Miss Hale observed them kissing. But it is not as though the blush is a result of being censured by Miss Hale, far from it. There is actually a hint, quite distinct (the smile, her fingers on the flowers, the lingering emphasis of her speech), that Miss Hale has drawn pleasure from watching them kiss. And as if to confirm this, Miss Hale looks up and observes, with quiet delight, the colour on Catherine's cheeks. At the same time, Catherine catches the hint of colour on Miss Hale's cheeks, and for a moment they are two girls, exchanging confidences, vague, allusive confidences, hinting at forbidden things.

They part. Catherine begins her duties (the house and Miss Hale's cottage, which has an inside adjoining door leading into the main building, being empty apart from Miss Hale and Catherine). But later, as Catherine is finishing, Miss Hale joins her in the hall before she leaves. 'If you like, you can bring your book of poems to me. My friend is coming up today.'

Catherine smiles, surprised and relieved that the incident in the rose garden has now, it seems, been put behind them. 'Oh, yes. I will. I will indeed.'

'Good, he will be happy to sign it.'

'That's very kind of him.'

'Oh, but he *is* kind.' Here Miss Hale pauses for a moment, looking out over the garden. 'A lot more kind than people know. Everybody thinks him cold and distant.'

'Do they?' Catherine asks, aware, possibly for the first time, that she has never contemplated the possibility of his being cold or distant or warm or near. He has always been, quite simply, his poems. And a certain kind of photograph, the sort of photographs taken of writers that always make them look, well, above being cold or warm or distant or near.

'Yes, they do. They think him difficult to know. Like a sort of priest who's impossible to get a smile out of. Severe, I suppose. And that's when they even think of him as human at all, as apart from a sort of Westminster Abbey on legs.'

At this point, Catherine's eyes pop. This is exactly, word for word, Daniel's description of him. Has Miss Hale overheard their conversations somehow, as she, indeed, observed their kisses? And is she slyly letting on that she knows more than she says? Or did Daniel simply get the phrase from somewhere, and was the impression he gave of just having this happy knack of coming up with phrases like that an act? Luckily for Catherine, Miss Hale has briefly turned her attention to a flower in the bowl, twisting its stalk round to create a more harmonious arrangement.

'But that's not what I see,' she says, returning to Catherine. 'That's not my friend. He's really like those cats that sit all prim and proper on a garden bench and look as if they don't want to know you. Until you stroke their chins and they roll over on their backs because all along they were just waiting to be touched.' She smiles, almost as if in the act of stroking her friend's chin, implying that it's all in the way you stroke them, and, in having an instinct for knowing these things. 'They call him cold. But he's nothing of the sort.'

There is a pause and Catherine doesn't know if she should stay or go. It is awkward. Even though Miss Hale (putting some finishing touches to the bowl of flowers) is choosing to tell her all these private things, there is a part of Catherine that feels as though she shouldn't, all the same, be hearing any of this — as if they are private matters related by someone in a moment of weakness and that will be regretted later by both the confessor and the listener. Moreover, the silence is made more awkward by the sense of moment that comes with it. Miss Hale, Catherine senses, is not simply pausing for breath, she is, Catherine is convinced, on the brink of some confession and pausing for effect. And Catherine is not sure that she really wants to hear. But, of course, she is one of Miss Hale's girls now and she is about to receive a confidence.

'They'll also tell you that he has no instincts, no gift for affection, or even love. But don't believe it. You are eighteen and no doubt think that love is all adoring eyes and touch and market-stall kisses. And so it is, at eighteen. But there are different kinds of love.' She turns from the bowl to Catherine. 'As you get older, you come to understand that people can have deep bonds that are quite … different from what this world today calls love.' Then she smiles and clasps her hands together, as if to say that the matter is now concluded. Possibly even conceding that she may have spoken a little too freely. For until now, Catherine notes, Miss Hale has always spoken of her 'special' friend, or having known someone who did such and such, or had such and such inflicted upon him – like a bad marriage, or a wicked woman who continues to cling when she has no right to any more. But today she has spoken, quite specifically, about 'her' friend. As Catherine is asking herself why, she is remembering the scene in the rose garden. Did the ceremony – and Catherine has to remind herself that Miss Hale has absolutely no knowledge of her and Daniel witnessing the event – seal the love that she has just spoken of? And, for all the formal language that came with that declaration of love (and this is what it seems to Catherine), Miss Hale has as good as told her that she and her friend share the kind of love that is above certain things, like adoring eyes and touch and kisses. And it's not simply the right and proper acknowledgment of the fact that he is married (albeit separated); it has been said in such a way that implies they wouldn't descend to everyday love anyway. That they are above all of that. There is, it seems, young love – all kisses and burning flushes – that is over almost before it has been registered by the senses, and there is the love that rises above kisses and burning flushes, which lasts in the way that deep friendships last. But it is not, it seems, the kind of love that 'goes to bed', which, for Catherine, is the logical end of all their ardent ways. No, 'ardent' isn't their word as it is Catherine and Daniel's. Miss Hale and her friend have another kind of love, and, presumably, another word. At least this is the way Catherine takes it, and she is immediately puzzled because, among other things, some part of her is, well, almost shocked. And, at the same time, she also realises that she would be less shocked, in fact, not shocked at all but even happy, to learn that theirs was an affair like any other affair, a romance that followed the usual ways of romance. A romance that exuberantly sheds its clothes and goes to bed. Why else would Catherine have willed them on to happiness in the rose garden? So that they could rise above all the things that she was willing them towards? No, so that they should be lovers and do all the things that lovers do. But not Miss Hale and her special friend. They had, she had as much as informed Catherine with practised casualness, found a different kind of love. And the ring she wears, which Catherine has just noticed (and which she could almost be wearing in the way that a nun wears a ring), bears testimony to that love.

I saw you, Miss Hale's smile is saying, her hands still clasped; I saw you and your ardent ways in the market, impulsive as young love always is, and Catherine can't help but feel, once again, that Miss Hale drew a bitter-sweet pleasure from observing them. And at the same time there is a hint of something else. Don't imagine, her smile might be saying, don't imagine that is all there is to love. One loves as one can. I too love, she could be saying. I too love, even if it is not your ardent love of market-stall kisses.

Is this what her smile is saying? Is it a simple declaration of a pure love, a chaste love, that has been sworn to secrecy but which can't be kept secret because it is too vast for Miss Hale to keep in? Is it a declaration – albeit oblique, formal and implied – of the love that they had celebrated in the secrecy of the rose garden, away from the prying eyes of the world, the evidence of which was consigned to earth where it would have remained buried and secret forever? But, as much as they were pledged to secrecy, has Miss Hale felt, in the end, the overwhelming need to tell someone – and is that someone Catherine, a young woman she would never see again after this summer and autumn, who knows nothing of London literary society, and who could surely tell no one of any conceivable importance? Is this what this odd communication of silences and suggestive smiles is all about? Moreover, Catherine is, of course, one of her girls and bound to keep all knowledge passed on to her in strict confidence. The muse is restless, perhaps not content to remain a shadow, silent and forever in the background, where muses quietly go when their job is done.

And as much as she has declared her love, this muse's love, which is different by being above things, timeless, like the poetry it sparks into life, Catherine retains the lingering sensation of the blush, the hint of colour on Miss Hale's cheeks, and the unmistakable feeling that Miss Hale took slightly more pleasure from watching Daniel and her kiss than might be expected. For what happens, Catherine is silently asking the figure standing by the bowl of autumn flowers, what happens when he doesn't need you any more because he's got you stoppered in a bottle, and all he has to do to have you back is to lift the cork and inhale the essence of you? What happens when all you have left is the love letter but not the lover? What happens then? Do you watch young lovers kiss in the twilight at market stalls and remember what it was to be eighteen?

Did this muse, did Miss Hale, not only want to step out of the shadows that her role demanded of her but also into the ordinariness of ordinary love, which she hovered over like a bird after a long journey, eyeing land? A destination longed for, and tantalisingly close, but never to be nested in.

The conversation seemingly over, Catherine turns to the door to leave. But it is then that Miss

Hale slumps onto a chair and invites Catherine to do likewise.

'Ah, so good to have the house to ourselves. All of it.'

'Yes.' Catherine sits, nodding.

'Not that I'm not grateful to my aunt and uncle for all they've done. They've been wonderful guardians. But it is good to have it to ourselves, isn't it? Last night we dined with friends of my aunt and uncle. And the night before. And, of course, they are dear. And their friends. And all the small talk that friends share, which can be interesting or a little annoying depending on the talk and the evening and you.'

Catherine nods again, agreeing that all this is so, though more perplexed than anything by this sudden inclusiveness.

'Company is good, but sometimes we can have rather too much of it. Don't you agree?'

'Sometimes. Yes.'

'Like the town. It *is* pretty. And I do feel like I'm living in a travel brochure come to life – but it's small, don't you find? Confining after a while.'

Catherine, who is sitting more on the edge of her seat rather than on it, nods again, though she is not sure where all this is leading.

'If you are born into small-town country life, no doubt it comes naturally. But you're not, are you?'

'No.'

'Nor I. We're city people who like the escape of these places. But not to live in.'

'No.'

'Do you have any plans for when you finish school?' It is said as if to imply whatever the plan may be, it is to be hoped it will get her out of the town as much as anything else.

'Yes. I'd like …' and here Catherine hesitates, sure that what she is about to say will just sound silly. 'I'd like to go to a university. It's a sort of dream, I suppose.' She sighs, her weight now sinking into the seat.

'But these things happen. Like your young man. Daniel, isn't it?'

'Yes. But he's very bright. Once you get past all the skylarking, he's very bright indeed.'

'But so are you, Catherine. Trust me, after years of teaching, I know how to tell the bright girls from the rest. They announce themselves. And you, Catherine, announce yourself.'

'Thank you,' Catherine says, a trace of a blush returning. She almost adds 'Miss Hale', but decides against it in the context of this newfound intimacy.

'I always tell my girls – the bright ones – to believe in themselves. To have dreams. And to be bold in their dreaming. It's odd how so many bright girls don't, you know. Odd, how so many choose the conventional when so many have been born for far more than that.'

Miss Hale then rises and goes to the window and stares out over the garden as she had the previous morning. 'These towns are nice – but to live in? Sometimes it's so hard just to get away, don't you find?'

'Yes.' Catherine laughs, as if to say she knows this only too well.

'You and your young man, for instance. You must find it difficult to get away, to be some place without the whole town watching.'

Catherine stares back, knowing full well that she is not at all in control of the conversation, a conversation that still puzzles her. And now she is simply not sure what Miss Hale means. The town watching? Watching what, she thinks? But she nods in response all the same, because the observation, overall, is true. It is hard to go anywhere without the sense of somebody watching.

And then, as if reading Catherine's mind, Miss Hale says, 'Of course, there are the fields. But they're for sheep, aren't they?'

Here Catherine laughs out loud, awkward but genuinely amused at the observation. And Miss Hale breaks into a smile, pleased, it seems, with the sound of a young woman's laughter in the house.

'For the sheep,' Miss Hale goes on, 'or the girls who don't announce themselves. Or rather, shall we say, announce themselves in the wrong way altogether.'

It doesn't occur to Catherine to think the statement snobbish or prim because she agrees with Miss Hale – this is exactly what she thinks. And to pronounce Miss Hale a snob (as Daniel would), she would have to include herself as well.

'No,' Miss Hale continues, 'these towns can be so confining. When I saw you and your young man at the market yesterday evening, I thought – and I hope you don't mind my saying so –'

And Catherine shakes her head – too readily, she realises, for she doesn't even know what the woman is going to say or where on earth this conversation is leading.

'I thought … It must be difficult for them.'

This is a different Miss Hale again. Catherine knows the refined Miss Hale, even the prim Miss Hale. And she has also glimpsed the blunt Miss Hale who once liked you but doesn't any more and drops the social niceties, as well as having witnessed the theatrical Miss Hale who lets herself go and subtly alludes to things that she can't possibly tell you. Now, there is this other Miss Hale. Not the Miss Hale who hints at different kinds of love at the different stages of one's life, but the Miss Hale who seems quite comfortable talking about sheep paddocks and the kinds of girls who use them.

And as Catherine nods she remembers once again that Miss Hale had been watching Daniel and her from a distance, that she had witnessed their kissing in the open, a market-stall kiss that Miss Hale had taken a certain pleasure in watching. More pleasure, quite possibly, than one might expect. But this time Catherine does not blush, for she now suspects that she has experienced something that Miss Hale hasn't, or might once have.

Miss Hale then turns from the view out the window. 'You don't mind my saying this, do you?'

'No, I don't mind at all.' And Catherine adds, a little coyly, 'It's true.'

'I simply want you to understand that I appreciate these things. I was eighteen once, too.'

There it is again, Catherine observes, that note of regret. That sense of a long-ago garden, a young woman in another age, a young man, flowers flung to the ground, and that sense of something done badly, or not done at all. A memory, come down through the years, its power to haunt undiminished, for Miss Hale seems, quite genuinely, and it is not an act, to have slipped, irresistibly, into another time and place.

And it is while she is lost in that memory that Catherine decides to rise from her seat and excuse herself. As she rises, Miss Hale turns.

'Oh, I kept you too long.'

'Not at all.' And Catherine means it. She would gladly stay on, but just when it appears that the conversation is finally at an end, Miss Hale suddenly remembers something. 'Oh, but wait. I've something for you.' She rushes upstairs to the connecting door, while Catherine waits downstairs in the drawing room, observing the view from the window, half expecting to see a young woman and a young man, in the clothes of another age, standing in the garden.

'Here.' Miss Hale is back, a little breathless, holding a small wrapped package. 'These are for you. I bought them for myself, but decided afterwards that they belonged to a younger woman than I am now. And, you and I, we are the same height. I think you'll find they fit.' And here Miss Hale smiles as she passes the package over to Catherine, who thanks her profusely for the gift, without knowing, or even possibly caring, what it is. It is a gift from Miss Hale to one of her girls. An affirmation that Catherine is one of those girls who announce themselves, and that Miss Hale is watching over.

It is only when she is back home in her room that she dares to open the package, that she dares to pull the purple wrapping from the gift. And when she holds the gift aloft, a faint, quizzical smile lights her face. Stockings. Expensive. French. By English standards, adventurous. Certainly not the stockings that a middle-aged drama teacher from Boston would normally be seen wearing. In fact, Catherine is not exactly sure that *she* can be seen wearing them. Of course, she will be. Given the right time, and the right place.

But what a thing? The thought of Miss Hale even

buying them, let alone contemplating wearing them, is intriguing, for it opens up the possibility that there may be another side, *many* other sides, to Miss Hale altogether. Catherine falls back on the bed, running the material through her fingers, that faint, quizzical smile still lighting her face. Who would have expected that? What a thing. What a thing, indeed.

A deserted laneway isn't quite a sheep paddock, nor does it possess the privacy of a room of their own, but it is, nonetheless, where they stop. Catherine is backed up against a wall. Her arms are around Daniel's neck and her fingers are digging into his hair, which he swears needs cutting but which she'd rather left long. Her mouth is glued to his, her tongue, like a life-form unto itself, has been let loose inside his mouth, its tip darting here and there. She seems to be taking in mouthfuls of him, and he of her. She never knew until this summer that kissing could be this delirious, have such power, to make you forget or just not care that there's a world of people and houses and streets out there; everything (their lips, tongues, fingers and limbs) has given itself over to these ardent ways of theirs.

And just as their lips are glued to each other, so are their bodies. His knee is in between her legs, pressing deep into her. In the language of the street and the schoolyard, this, she knows, is what's called a knee-trembler. The girls at the various schools she's attended (and she's been to five) have talked of such things in a way that was both alarming and fascinating, but she had never experienced the thing until this summer. Her knowledge of boys and girls and what happens between them has been picked up in the schoolyard and through the books for and about young women and what happens in bedrooms, books that are circulated around the class, having been pilfered or ferreted out of a parent's drawer or off a bedside bookshelf by some enterprising girl for both her benefit and everybody else's as well – by one of those girls who do it, or say that they've done it. They're odd things, these pages from manuals, with odd words and phrases that she and most of the girls at the school can't help but laugh at because they're funny, and also because they're just a bit scary too – and laughing together makes them feel just a little bit less scared. But she's not laughing now, because along with his knee she can feel something else pressed against her as she leans back, eyes closed, against a wall, in a laneway, in a town, in a world, solar system … et cetera, et cetera. And if she thinks of the thing pressing against her, words such as 'penis' and 'member' and all the rest of those silly, bloody terms don't occur to her. She simply thinks of the thing as 'it'. If she thinks of it at all. For the one thing she has observed about moments such as these, when she looks back on them, is that she's usually not thinking. She's free of thinking. And it's puzzling that she should feel such joy at being free of thought because she loves thought. But she's also beginning to appreciate the sheer exhilaration of having all thought wiped away by touch. Certainly, at the moment, words don't matter. Like Daniel, she's all touch, no thought.

And Daniel, his mouth glued to hers, tongue to tongue, feels as though he is merging with her, almost as though they have collided and stuck, which is pretty much what has happened this summer, and what happened just a few moments ago when they found the laneway deserted, and, without even catching each other's eyes, collided, and wound up pressed against the wall with their mouths glued to each other. Did he start it; did she? Did she draw him in to her, or did he take himself there? He did, she did, they did.

But as much as the world seems to have been deliriously obliterated, they are suddenly jerked back into it.

'Gotta come up for air sometime.'

Two men pass, and their voices, their footsteps on the stone path and the sounds of the high street just up to their right, bring the unwanted world back. But Catherine and Daniel don't look up, and they don't acknowledge the two men. They look down instead, waiting for them to pass, Catherine softly muttering something about why don't people just leave other people alone. And it is true, Daniel is thinking, why can't they? But because they are in a public place, these two men assume it to be a public matter, which they wouldn't, of course, if Catherine and Daniel were arguing instead of kissing. No, if they were arguing or fighting these two men would look the other way and pretend it wasn't happening. But, somehow, the act of kissing in public, the act of, as the phrase goes, 'making love' in public, is a public matter, and so the men say stupid things about coming up for air. And, as much as Catherine is angered by their intrusion, she is also annoyed by their lack of imagination. These two men have interrupted a delirious moment, jolted Daniel and her back into the world, with a cliché. And not only, Catherine concludes, does the cliché reflect on the men who used it, it reflects on her and Daniel as well. They have not only been interrupted by a cliché, they have been cheapened by it.

As the two men pass into the distance and out on to the high street, Catherine and Daniel move apart and hand in hand they stroll up the laneway towards the high street. It is then that Catherine tells him about her conversation with Miss Hale the previous morning – the conversation, and the gift that followed.

'What?' Daniel has stopped and is staring with incredulity at Catherine. 'Don't you think that's a little, well, odd?'

Catherine nods. 'A little,' she says, taking a private delight in the incredulous look still on Daniel's face. She could have said more than this. Yes, it is odd. Decidedly so. Funny old thing, and so on. But she didn't say this; she said 'a little' odd. And she means it. There is, she tells herself, an understanding between her and Miss Hale. She is, after all, one of Miss Hale's girls. And, although she tells Daniel things, she knows she can never quite explain to him just what it means to be one of Miss Hale's girls. For there is, she knows, an element of the secret, of the exclusive society, that can never be fully communicated to someone else outside that society. And so although Daniel looks at her with incredulity, there is that part of Catherine that accepts the gift as any of Miss Hale's girls would – that part of her that looks upon it, not so much as an odd act, or even an eccentric one, but as a compliment, a gift given by one adult to another.

'She says,' Catherine continues as they follow the pathway, 'that there are different kinds of love. And as we grow, love changes.'

'She would.'

'That's cruel.'

'It's true. What are they, these different kinds of love?'

'She never says anything directly. She never just comes out and says things. She always seems to be in some sort of play – the sort of play where no one comes out and says what they really want to say.'

'So she means the old sex thing.'

There is a kind of smugness to the way Daniel says this, and Catherine's immediate instinct is to take

Miss Hale's side, for it is the kind of comment, and the kind of turn of phrase (a smart, studenty one, which is unlike Daniel), that demands sides be taken. And so she does. 'What do you mean, the old sex thing?'

'That's the way these people talk. The sex thing. The woman thing. They're still children. So what she means is they don't do it because that's beneath them these days, but they do have this wonderful spiritual thing instead of the sex thing.'

'Do you have to say it like that?'

'But it's true. She's just an old maid. Bit more style than most, but an old maid. And he's just as likely to be an old queer who doesn't know what to do with himself. They're made for each other. A funny bunch, if you ask me.'

'That's awful. You don't mean all that? And even if you do, do you have to say it like that?'

Catherine, knowing that Daniel, like her, is probably just angry at being interrupted and cheapened by a cliché, says this just as they hit the high street. With people suddenly around them and within earshot, they stop talking even though she would dearly love to go on and tell Daniel just how much he annoys her when he talks like that (and she's surprised because he rarely does). But he's also annoyed her because what he's said is hurtful. She is not so much hurt herself but hurt on Miss Hale's behalf. It is all part of taking sides. For her heart is still going out to Miss Hale, still urging her on to happiness.

At the same time, Daniel (and Catherine is fully aware of this because Daniel has told her) knows something – not much, but something – about this 'old sex thing' because he has done it. He is, after all, twenty-two. He's been at Cambridge for four years and they have girls there. And, of course, he's told her with the self-satisfied air of the prankster who got away with one of his finest stunts that it's difficult to get in and out of the women's rooms without being caught, but that it can be done if you know how. And he has. Once. Up the window and out the window on a fireman's rope. He's told her this, and although he might boast about the trick, he didn't about the girl like any of the other local boys would (and that's another reason she never wants to be caught in the open because everybody talks around here). No, he's told her because he thinks she ought to know. Just as he's told her that he expected everything to be different afterwards, but it wasn't. Everybody else, he'd thought, had this knowledge – and he didn't. But, once he'd done it, he would. Only, when it was all over (and Daniel has not told her that it was all over in a flash and that the first thing he'd done was apologise to the girl – who'd told him not to be silly), he didn't feel any different. This knowledge that he'd fully expected to come with the whole thing failed to arrive. So, when he talks about the sex thing the way he just has, he's not pretending to know anything much more than Catherine – and she knows this because Daniel doesn't put on airs and doesn't pretend to be things he's not. But still, he annoyed her just then, and as they cross the road to a quiet street (on their way to a music recital in the parish church, where a quartet will play Beethoven), she continues as if they hadn't stopped. 'Well, do you?'

'Do I what?'

'Have to say it like that.'

'Would you rather I didn't quite say it, the way they don't quite say it in plays? Besides, if she's so happy, why does she tell you all this? And why does she give you stockings?'

'That's just it – she's not happy.'

Ten minutes earlier, their mouths had been glued together; now the church is upon them. Pausing at the front of it, they acknowledge their shared impatience of the town with a brief flash of the eyes – the town and all the silly people who come along and say silly things just when you wish they'd shut up. But, all the same, they must have lingered longer in that laneway than they thought, for they've only just made the lunchtime recital and enter as the doors are closing.

It is a modest affair, a quartet of musicians from the surrounding towns, probably students, but a surprisingly large attendance. Larger, Catherine suspects, than they might usually get for the Sunday-morning service. She puts it down to a town in which nothing much happens and the powers of the church to draw on its parishioners. But although it's a modest affair, the size of the church (almost a cathedral, really – with its high ceiling and high windows) adds a touch of grandeur to the occasion. She's rarely been here and is distracted by the place. There is an early-autumn chill in the air inside the church that the sun has not yet dispelled, but the light coming in from the stained-glass windows makes everything glow. Like another world, which (it occurs to Catherine for the first time) might well be the point of those windows – not so much the stories they tell or the saints they depict but the glow they create. A touch of heaven, a hint of things to come.

Daniel stands awkwardly in the church. He is only there because she is. And for the music. He is well aware of Lenin's famous remark about music and listening to Beethoven, and how it turns you into a sentimentalist and distracts you from the job at hand – which, for Lenin, was nothing less than transforming the world. While he may think in grand historical terms (Daniel, like so many of his fellow students, talks of the dialectics of History as a scientist might talk of gravity), he has no such personal ambitions. Besides, he loves music. All music. Popular songs, classical. He may, he smiles to himself, be standing under the high beams of an Anglican church, but he is catholic in his tastes. He doesn't know much about Beethoven string quartets, but he is keen to hear this group of what look like students (already seated at the top of the aisle) perform, the poster on the door says, a Quartet in A Minor. Major is happy, minor is sad. Daniel, whose musical knowledge is limited, knows this, and prepares himself for a sad experience.

There is no charge but Catherine drops coins into the collection bowl as they pass it round – for the musicians, she assures Daniel, not the church. As they are about to take their seats (most of the spaces bearing plaques informing everyone that Mr and or Mrs So-and-So made the pew possible with their good works and money), Catherine catches sight of the back of Miss Hale's head. And almost as soon as she has done that, she sees, in profile, the beak-like nose of Miss Hale's special friend as he turns to speak to her. They are only a few rows in front and there is no mistaking it. As soon as she sees them, she nudges Daniel and nods in their direction.

Then a hush falls across the church, and, after a brief introduction, the quartet begins. And, straight away the sad sounds for which he'd prepared himself flow from the four players (three young men and a young woman) and rise to the ceiling. And Daniel, who has not attended many concerts, is struck by the power of live performance, the almost physical power of the music these performers make together, and the sight of the aged wood of the instruments and the trilling wire and gut of the strings, all adding something … something immediate and urgent to the performance that he did not expect. Immediately, he knows that Lenin was right, but the thought is no sooner in his head than it is out, as the music (both edgy and sad, it seems to him, like two opposite halves of a personality trying to resolve themselves) sweeps him up and transports him, the way, he will note afterwards, these things do. Catherine, likewise, forgets all about Daniel, the kisses like none she's ever known, the sex thing and the people who interrupt you with their clichés when you wish they'd just mind their own business and gives herself up to the music, which lifts her too and takes her somewhere else that has a hint of heaven about it. Together, they are here, in this church, and they are not here, and, while it may be midday outside, inside they are existing, Catherine fancies, in no particular time at all.

When it is over and the final notes have fallen to the ground and they are all back on Earth again, she looks around, still in a drowsy half-sleep. Gradually, in twos and threes and fours, the audience rises and slowly files out through the open door as if everyone were in the same daze. It is only then, as the church begins to empty, that Catherine remembers Miss Hale and her friend, and notes that they are still seated, staring straight ahead where the musicians are now packing up their instruments. Their music has warmed everyone for a short time, but that early-autumn chill is still in the air. Catherine's immediate impulse is to join the exiting audience and to be outside when Miss Hale and her friend emerge so that she might catch

Miss Hale's eye, greet her, and, as society demands, Miss Hale will introduce her friend. With this in mind, she nudges Daniel once again, nods towards the door, and they both rise.

Daniel leaves her when they are outside, having promised to help his father with the lunchtime shoppers as he had often done as a boy. Not having told Catherine his plans, she is not happy to be standing about alone. In fact, she wavers on the path (the mossy teeth of occasional gravestones sticking up at all angles on the lawn beside her) in the shadow of the giant church tower that looks more like a castle keep, not sure now whether to go or stay. But matters are soon taken out of her hands when Miss Hale and her friend emerge from the church and stand framed in the doorway. Other members of the audience are still gathered on the lawn outside, discussing the performance before going their separate ways, but a single young woman stands out in the mostly middle-aged attendance, and Miss Hale notices her and smiles in recognition straight away. Then Miss Hale takes her friend by the arm and leads him directly to her, and as Catherine watches them approach, her heartbeat quickens, and she is wondering if she might not have been better off leaving with Daniel. Miss

Hale, almost as if having remembered that they are in public view and ought to be careful, relinquishes her hold on her friend's arm, but, nonetheless, smiles in that same way that she does when offering up some detail about her friend, a detail that may or may not, in some people's minds, amount to gossip. But Catherine is only vaguely aware of this, for it is the imposing figure of Miss Hale's friend that so occupies her eyes and mind. Afterwards she will put the experience more satisfactorily in order but at the moment she is aware of his height and his stoop. He is taller and more stooped (it seems) for being directly in front of her, inclining towards her in the way that tall people do when meeting someone, or when engaged in conversation. And Daniel's joke (if it is Daniel's joke) about his being a sort of Westminster Abbey on legs has never rung so true, for there is something of the edifice about Miss Hale's friend that makes Catherine feel as though she is standing in the shadow of a public building instead of the church tower.

'Tom, this is the young woman I told you about. Catherine, this is Tom.'

Catherine is only vaguely aware of Miss Hale's voice and is only vaguely aware of nodding in her direction, for she is still standing in the shadow of a public building, not a human being. Until she meets his eyes, that is, and Catherine is shocked to realise that Miss Hale's friend is handsome. Far more so, it seems to her, than in his photographs. Some people *do* photograph badly (like Daniel) and you never realise just how handsome or attractive they are until you meet them. Yes, he's handsome – and she had not expected this – in the way that a matinee actor might be handsome. The sort of face that girls of a certain type, a certain type such as Catherine, might even get a crush on. And as much as she smothers the thought, it is there still, and a slight blush colours her cheeks. And it is then she notes that Miss Hale is smiling, not so much at her, as upon her, as if, in the blush and the wide eyes of Catherine, she is reading every single thought that is passing through her mind, because, at that moment, Catherine is sure her mind is an open book. And, as for 'Tom' … That's just not on. And it wouldn't matter how many times she met him, she could never call him 'Tom'. Always Mr Eliot. Only Mr Eliot.

'Catherine,' Miss Hale continues, turning her smile to her friend, 'is an avid reader of yours, Tom. She has a book for you to sign.'

'Gladly.'

'Thank you.'

It is then that he stretches out his hand and she realises she will be called upon to clutch it in greeting. And it is like shaking hands with History, even down to the coldness of his hand. As if the thinnest of thin blood were running through it. It is firm enough; it is brief. It is the handshake of a public man used to shaking the hands of strangers. And then it is over. He and Miss Hale excuse themselves. They are gone. And it is not the matinee looks of Miss Hale's friend that linger on, nor the stoop of the public building, but the coolness of his skin as he shook her hand. And she can't believe, as she watches him take Miss Hale's hand as they walk away, that this is also what Miss Hale feels, or surely she would fling his hand away from her, like a bouquet of flowers to the ground.

But, just as she thinks this, she hears it. A boom, yes, a boom. His head is thrown back and the boom of his laughter shatters the afternoon autumn stillness and quiet, and all heads turn to the hearty soul who possesses such laughter. For it is the kind of laughter, Catherine can't help but think, that comes from someone with a warm heart, albeit cool hands. And she remembers the early-autumn chill in the church, and concludes that, no, Miss Hale does not feel the same cold hand that she did.

That evening, and it is a luminous Wednesday evening, Catherine sits on a bench in the high street near the bus stop at the old marketplace, waiting for Daniel. She has a good view of the street from here. Down to where Daniel's father has his shop (and at which Daniel has been all afternoon) and up to the top of the high street to the house that Miss Hale and her aunt and uncle have rented for the summer.

The music, and its effect on her, has lingered all afternoon; as she walked home, as she read, as she dressed to go out tonight. So much so that before coming here to meet Daniel she wandered back to the church. She had time on her hands, the chill that had been in the air earlier in the day had gone, and it was a good time for a walk – a warm evening, a glowing sky. Besides, inside the church the memory of the music would be stronger, she thought, and so it was. Unexpected pleasures, she mused, standing at the back of the church (for although there was no service in progress, there were two other people in the church, possibly praying, possibly visiting like herself), are all the more memorable for being unexpected. The memory of the music was no stronger but she could visualise the scene again and lingered a while.

Then, just as she was about to leave, she noticed the man seated a few rows in front of her. He was familiar, but why? And then she noticed the beak-like profile, the hair combed back, smooth and flat, with a parting down one side, not unlike his Mr Prufrock, and she stopped in her tracks. He was silent, perfectly still. It was a large church but she could see, when she looked more closely, that his lips were moving. And she realised, with something of a shock, that he was praying. Catherine didn't go to church and never really thought much about God, and it occurred to her that she'd quite possibly never really observed, close at hand, someone praying. And just as the music had had unexpected power, watching Miss Hale's friend pray was a strangely powerful experience, even moving. And she couldn't say why – not to herself, not then, and not now as she sits on a bench at the bus stop – except to say that it was the almost imperceptible movement of the lips, in the midst of all that stillness. And was there the faintest of whispering or not? He was, she concluded, almost happy. And, at that moment, she had willed them both on to happiness, Miss Hale and her friend, as she had in the rose garden. But she was, nonetheless, vaguely troubled by the image of Mr Eliot. There was something, well, almost wrong about Mr Eliot kneeling before anyone or anything, even a god. No, especially a god. She had to stifle the impulse to tell him to get up, that *her* Mr Eliot did not kneel. But more troubling, and here she was thinking of Miss Hale, was the distinct impression that, inside that church, he was a man who might, like anybody, enjoy human company, but who could, if pressed, get by without it.

Now, on the bench, she mulls over the words of Miss Hale (no doubt, at this moment, back in the house with her aunt and uncle, doing whatever they do at this time of day); the words of Miss Hale, these different kinds of love, and her friend (who seemed so complete, so contained, and yes, even happy, as he knelt in the private world of prayer), as well as the whole idea of love, of being eighteen, the sex thing, and Daniel, who is leaving in a week. And, just as she has had the sensation of stepping into and being part of a story for some time now, she now has the feeling that it is not entirely accidental that they have all crossed paths. All four. Strains of the music come back to her from the concert, four players, four melodies, weaving in and out of one another until they come to an abrupt halt and we know that a movement has been completed. There is a pause in the air and a lingering silence hovers over the square, the lingering silence that comes between the end of one part and the beginning of another.

She looks up the high street and notices the old bus groaning towards her, passing Miss Hale's house (who may well be observing the same bus), and imagines her friend, no longer kneeling, but strolling back to meet her. Then she turns her head as she rises, wondering where on earth Daniel could possibly be (they are going to the cinema at a town nearby), and sees him approaching, smiling, eyes alight as if contemplating some little prank, and she is aware of her whole mood lifting as she rises, instantly forgetting that world of high churches where lips that would kiss form prayers instead, and goes to meet him, their bodies, their mouths, coming together magnetically.

Twilight begins to settle over the town as the bus carrying them lumbers out. The sky, the trees, the sheep fields glow. And so, it seems to Catherine, do they. She knows, beyond doubt, that whatever Miss Hale and her friend may have settled upon, whatever has brought them back together, and whatever has brought her all this way over land and oceans and time, far from her school and away from her girls, to a small English town for the summer, whatever has done all that and whatever it is that sustains them, she would give it all away, just to be Catherine at this very moment, holding Daniel's hand with her heart beating like mad.

PART THREE

A Time for Taking Sides
September, 1934

Has the letter been left out on the hall-stand for Catherine to read? So that there will be no need for anybody to ask or answer questions, so that the mood in the house can be observed and understood and her visit be as brief as possible because nobody is really in the mood for talking. After stepping into the hallway, with the book in hand, to be signed on this bright Thursday morning, the first thing she saw was the letter lying on the hall-stand (with what appears to be a publisher's card pinned to the top of it, as though the letter itself has been passed on via another party). Was it left out so she could read it, or would she be prying?

Miss Hale, after a brief greeting, takes the book from her and leaves Catherine alone in the hall beside the stand upon which the letter sits, and Catherine, after asking herself if she dares, can't help but read the thing.

Will T.S. Eliot please return to his home
68 Clarence Gate Gardens
which he abandoned Sept. 17th, 1932.
Keys with WLJ

It is short enough to be taken in at a glance, yet long enough to be a story in itself. And Catherine instantly recognises that it is a very sad story for the person who wrote it (presumably the wicked woman who clings to things long after she has any right to). But, as much as it tells a sad story, it is also, she assumes, a disturbing letter to receive, as the mood of the house instantly tells her: although the house itself would probably choose to call it 'awkward'. As she looks up from the letter and down the hall into the drawing room, she can make out Miss Hale whispering to her friend who is staring out a window, nodding as she speaks.

As is often the case when she is in this house, Catherine doesn't know whether to stay or go. The timing is all wrong and she is sure she is imposing on them at a particularly delicate moment. But just as she is about to raise her arm, just as she is about to signal to Miss Hale that the timing is all wrong and that she will leave and return another, more opportune, time, or not return at all (she doesn't really need the signature and should never have asked for it), just as she is about to signal all of this, Miss Hale's friend turns to her, and the transformation in his appearance shocks her into inertia. Gone is the face that emitted such booming, hearty laughter the day before, and upon which everybody turned and smiled, for it had been the happy sound of a hearty soul, the sort of sound that lights up other people's faces and lives, and lets them forget, or simply put in perspective their concerns for a moment. That face has gone now, along with the matinee looks and the twinkle in his eye (the same sort of twinkle that Catherine has seen in Daniel's eyes, just before he launches into some practical joke or other). And Catherine suspects that that lost happy face is the one that Miss Hale's friend would rather go through life wearing from now on: that after years of being Westminster Abbey on legs he wants to live and laugh, and possibly be allowed to fall in love again, just like anybody else. Maybe even waste his time in idle pursuits, for he has the look of someone whose life, whose days, even whose hours, have, for year upon year, been organised like a school timetable. And you can only live like that for so long. So perhaps he'd like to throw some of his timetabled days away reading Sherlock Holmes, even memorising whole pages for a party trick; he looks the sort. But it is all proving to be extremely difficult. No, the face that yesterday had emitted such booming laughter is gone, and the one that now turns to her is transformed utterly. Above all, it is the eyes. No trace of a twinkle, no hint of a prank. And it is not just this sadness that she sees there, but something else. For the face that he shows her is not only the face of someone upon whom sadness has fallen, but someone who is also frightened. His eyes are opened wide, and a dark mood, almost physical in its intensity, seems to be emanating from him. Even more than frightened, and Catherine now remembers Miss Hale's words (that seemed so melodramatic at the time) about goddesses, and hauntings and Furies, and concludes that the fear she sees in the eyes of Miss Hale's friend is the fear of someone who sincerely believes himself damned to be haunted and pursued for life. And whereas she was once tempted to laugh at such an idea, she's not now. Nor, she is sure, is he acting. Or, if he is, he is an exceptional performer.

He then nods, a faint sense of recognition that says, yes, we have met before, and yes, I promised to sign your book 'gladly', if I recall correctly, and so I shall – but you'll forgive me if the gladness has gone from me for the time being. Then he looks down as Miss Hale hands him the book and he stares at it with a perplexed expression, almost as if looking upon the book for the first time and wondering who on earth the person was who wrote enough poems to fill a whole volume. Could it really have been him? But of course it was (albeit a sufficiently distant him to be someone else), and he quickly signs his name on the title page and hands it back to Miss Hale, nodding briefly in Catherine's direction before turning his gaze back upon the garden outside.

As Miss Hale returns, her face gives nothing away to Catherine. A promise has been made, and a promise has been kept. A duty dispatched. She has looked after one of her girls, and she hands back the book with the kind of controlled poise that suggests, without it being stated, that this is a trying moment. And it is then that Miss Hale looks down and sees the letter, open on the hall-stand for all the world to see, and, as she snatches it up, she looks abruptly back at Catherine, attempting to fathom if the thing has been read, has remained unread, or was even noticed. Catherine is quick to avert her eyes, and is aware of Miss Hale's enquiring gaze, but like the woman beside her, Catherine gives nothing away. And, from the corner of her eye, Catherine notices Miss Hale stuffing the letter into her pocket while she guides her to the door.

Again, Catherine is wondering, as she stands on the doorstep, saying goodbye to Miss Hale, was the note left out for her to read, and was the surprise of finding the letter open to the enquiring eyes of strangers another piece of performance – or had the news the letter contained been so disturbing that it had been dropped on the table in the hall and forgotten about until Miss Hale had returned the signed copy of her friend's poems and seen it lying there, exposed to the enquiring eyes of strangers such as Catherine.

Catherine turns to Miss Hale as she leaves. 'Thank you,' and adds, falling in with Miss Hale's coded language, 'tell your friend he is very kind.'

Miss Hale nods, the faintest trace of a smile. 'You'll forgive us if we don't ask you to stay, but it's been a – what shall we say? – an awkward morning.'

'Of course.' And with that she turns, following the curve of the high street down to the shops, leaving Miss Hale standing at the door, the faraway look in her eyes giving every impression that, although physically in the doorway, she is still living in another time and place, and whatever was left undone might yet be completed.

Later that morning in her room, Catherine is staring at the tobacco tin exhumed from the rose garden on what now seems to be such a distant day. Not the beginning of this autumn, but last autumn. Or the one before. She does not open the tin, but can hear the small metal object inside shift whenever she moves it. She doesn't open it because that would be snooping. It's bad enough that she's even in possession of the damned thing, but peering into the private life inside? That much she can control, and so she doesn't snoop. Like gossip, snooping is beneath the lady.

And while she is staring at the small tin (the name of a well-known brand of pipe tobacco printed on the lid), she is asking herself, what she can do. By which she means what can she do to help, given that she can find no way of giving back the tin, of retrieving the act of folly in the rose garden and restoring some part of Miss Hale's happiness. What can she do, not only to help Miss Hale and her friend without revealing the cause of their troubles, but to rid herself of the nagging guilt that, while not as intense as it was, is still, nonetheless, always there. Especially on mornings such as these when she feels her guilt all over again.

And then, as if in answer to her question, there is a knock on the door. Her mother is at the school preparing for the new term and Catherine opens the door to find a little girl from the town (whom she has seen about the place, but whose name she doesn't know) standing in front of her, a sealed envelope in her hands. The girl peers at her quizzically. She is clearly on an errand.

'Is your name Catherine?' she asks like an adult.

'Yes,' says Catherine, as if speaking to one.

It is then that the little girl thrusts the envelope into her hands.

'The American lady in the high street asked me to give you this.'

Catherine has no sooner taken the envelope than the girl is gone.

'Thank you,' she calls, and the girl waves without turning as she runs off, no doubt back to her friends with a small reward for her mission.

When Catherine opens the letter, she finds the briefest of messages.

'Can you please come? E.H.'

It doesn't say so, but the brevity of the note implies urgency, and so Catherine quickly returns to her room, puts the tin back in her drawer, and prepares herself to face the street, and Miss Hale for the second time that morning. Or should that be E.H.? There is, she notes, a certain satisfaction in the note being signed with her initials only, for the initials speak of one adult requesting the company and the help of another.

The door is opened soon after she knocks and Miss Hale ushers her into the house. 'Thank you for coming so quickly. Please, sit.'

Miss Hale's friend, Catherine notes immediately, has gone. Miss Hale is on edge. She is not herself. There is no hint of playing. She is not acting like someone on edge. She simply is. She sits opposite Catherine, her fingers tapping on the small table between them. One moment her eyes and mind are far away, the next she speaks as if inwardly having dispelled any doubts about saying what she is about to say. 'I have a request. You may accept or decline. It is entirely up to you. I will understand if you refuse. So, do *not* feel you must. It is simply a request.'

Catherine nods, puzzled, intrigued, even excited, but says nothing.

'Well.' Miss Hale nods in return, placing both hands on her knees, as if to say that she will come directly to the business at hand. 'As you know – as I have mentioned – my friend, my dear, dear friend, in his youth made a bad marriage. No one is to blame,' Miss Hale says, lifting her palms and her gaze to the heavens, 'but it was a marriage made in hell, all the same. And now my friend wishes to leave the marriage, only she won't let him. She is, as I have said, the type who clings long after she has any right to.' There is a brief pause as she looks down to the floor, slowly shaking her head from side to side. 'How, how indeed, do you leave someone who refuses to be left?'

Miss Hale lifts her head and eyes Catherine, gauging if the full import of what she is saying is being taken in, and, if so, what the girl is thinking.

'She follows him to his work. To official functions. She has even tried to post an advertisement in *The Times*, telling him to come home. Home?' Miss Hale raises her eyebrows as she says the word.

Catherine nods, knowing straight away that Miss Hale is referring to the letter left out on the hall-stand.

'She might even hire a detective. Who knows? The woman is obsessed.'

Catherine notes that the emphasis on that last word is not acted, but carries with it a whole summer, perhaps even years, of frustration.

'It must stop,' Miss Hale continues wearily, then looks down at a sealed envelope on the table, bites her lip, and stares directly back at Catherine.

'Will you take this to her?' she asks, indicating the envelope.

'Personally?'

'Yes.'

The eyes of Miss Hale give nothing away. She remains impassive. But, in spite of the steadiness of her gaze, in the silence that follows there is urgency in the air, the faintest hint of desperation of someone at the end of her tether, driven to such measures. A stranger in town, turning to the only person she can think of who might help her through this difficult time. And there is part of Catherine that feels that she herself has conjured up this request from Miss Hale, for in quietly asking herself the question 'What can I do?' just that morning, did she not call, and was her call not answered? And while others might reasonably reply that as much as they sympathise, it is, really, none of their business, Catherine cannot. For Catherine knows it *is* her business. And without even taking time to weigh it all up, she knows what must be done, and nods again, a second time. Yes, she will. Yes, she is, after all, one of Miss Hale's girls, and would never dream of letting her down any more than she would betray her trust. You need only, the nod says, you need only ask.

There is the most minute of sighs from Miss Hale before she continues. 'You may wonder why you have to. Why I simply cannot post the letter in question myself. But I do not want my friend to know and you must never breathe a word of it. It must be as though the letter never existed.' Here she fixes Catherine with an uncompromising stare to which Catherine nods twice this time. Taking the nods to be a pledge, Miss Hale goes on. 'He would be aghast if, even by the wildest of chances, anything ever got back to him. Perhaps humiliated. And that would be the end of the friendship. Do you understand the importance of this?'

'Yes.' Catherine cannot conceive of how anything could get back to her friend, but she can also see that

Miss Hale is in no condition to receive such assurances, and so lets it pass. She is thinking and talking the way people do when they've got themselves in a state. And so, while one part of Catherine is nodding and saying yes, another part recognises that Miss Hale is in a state and that what seems perfectly reasonable to her (this insistence that the letter be hand-delivered) isn't quite adding up. And although this sceptical side of Catherine will surface with greater clarity later on, at this particular moment it is Miss Hale's state of mind that preoccupies her. The distinct possibility that Miss Hale has got herself worked up and is not thinking things through clearly is pushed aside for now. For Catherine is one of Miss Hale's girls, and this is no time for quibbles or lessons in logic. Like the age itself, it is a time for taking sides.

'Yes,' Miss Hale hums, as if to say she chooses her girls well. 'I believe you do,' she continues. 'Besides, they would stamp the letter at the post office, and this woman will then know where it came from, and then where she may possibly find her husband. And he, of course, poor man, does not *want* to be found. That is the last thing he wants, and if I were to bring it upon him I would never forgive myself — whatever words of forgiveness he may offer.' She stops abruptly, as if the last words have been wrung from her. 'So you see it must be delivered by hand. She may have her suspicions as to where he may be found – and in whose company – in among the many towns in this popular spot, but suspicions and knowledge are two separate things.' Miss Hale stares out the window a moment. 'You may also be wondering why I don't go myself. That, however, would be to reveal myself,' and there is, to Catherine, more than a hint of someone tired of being in the shadows because she can't reveal herself, tired of being the woman no one speaks of because she's not here, tired of the game. 'Besides,' she goes on, 'sometimes things are best said in letters. People can get in the way.' She looks down at the letter in her hands. 'You will knock on the door. If she is not in, speak with Janes.'

'Who's that?'

'He's the servant. Have you got that?'

'And if she is in?'

'Then, if you can, bring her reply back with you. Though I don't hold out much hope. Still, it must be tried. Heaven only knows, we must try.'

There is a long pause and Miss Hale, whose carriage is always upright, especially when seated, slumps a little in her chair, as if to say that this whole wretched business is completely beneath her, beneath Catherine, beneath anybody with any sense of dignity, which, it is implied, the woman for whom the letter is intended clearly lacks.

'You may accept or decline, the choice is yours.'

'I'll do it,' Catherine says, in a manner that suggests she thought it was already decided and was never in doubt.

'You don't need to think it over?'

'No.'

'You're sure?'

'Positive.'

The relief is immediately evident on Miss Hale's face. 'Thank you, Catherine. Thank you. You have my gratitude.' And, just in case Catherine does not understand the significance of this, she adds: 'And, Catherine, I do not give my gratitude lightly.' She nods firmly, as if to say that with her gratitude comes her word, and with her word … everything. She then passes the letter to Catherine who notices immediately that the address on the envelope is the same she noticed in the letter this morning – the address to which T.S. Eliot should return, which is his home, and which he abandoned.

'You will need to go to London,' Miss Hale informs her, her voice matter-of-fact. 'Can you leave first thing in the morning?'

'Yes.'

'You've no appointments?'

'Appointments? Of course not.'

'You'll be gone the whole day.'

Catherine nods.

'What will you tell your mother?'

'I'll think of something.'

'Remember, not a word of this.'

'Not a word.'

Miss Hale then hands Catherine a second sheet of paper. It contains, Catherine sees immediately, a map and instructions. She will, Miss Hale informs her, need to travel to Paddington Station (adding that Catherine has more than likely made the trip before and probably doesn't need to be told). 'At Paddington you take the Underground. If you get confused, ask someone. You must take the Inner Circle, Catherine. The Inner Circle. And you get off at Baker Street. The map will guide you from there. It is walking distance. Do you understand?'

'Yes.'

'Do you need me to explain it again?'

'No, it is perfectly clear.'

Miss Hale gazes at her steadily for a moment, then nods. A nod that once more suggests that she, Miss Hale, chooses her girls well. And it is then that Miss Hale's tone changes completely, almost as though a thought has just occurred to her. 'Your young man leaves soon, does he not?'

'Yes.'

Miss Hale smiles faintly. 'When the days are few, the days are important.' She glances quickly in Catherine's direction. 'Perhaps we can find a way to make up for the lost time.'

Catherine can't imagine what she means, but replies, 'That's not necessary.'

'Naturally, I will pay for your tickets and any expenses.' She then hands over what Catherine knows is more than enough money. And there is also an unstated recognition, that, with money passing from one hand to another, with the exchange of notes, a contract has been sealed, and Catherine has the distinct sensation of becoming – what do they call it? – a hired hand. For the money brings with it a certain grubbiness. And, as Catherine registers this sensation herself, she sees in the eyes of Miss Hale the same thought, and with it the sentiment that the whole grubby business is beneath them both.

What Catherine didn't tell Miss Hale was that she had, in fact, never been to London. In their travels together, from city to town, in the different places her mother had taught and to which she had been taken, she had never been to London. In accepting the responsibility of delivering the letter, she had no intention of saddling Miss Hale with the concern, and possibly guilt, of knowing that her messenger had never been to the place to which she was required to go. It was also a matter of pride. For Catherine had long prided herself on being an independent spirit, and to decline Miss Hale's request out of sheer faint-heartedness went completely against the grain. Besides, she had the instructions and a map. The getting there would not be difficult. The difficulties, she feared, would begin *when* she got there.

She told her mother that evening that she would be gone the whole of the next day. Her mother asked where and Catherine told her.

'London? But, you've never been there.'

'Well then, it's time I went.'

When her mother asked why, Catherine lied (one of the few times she had ever lied to her mother) with a clear conscience. She mumbled something about books. Books she had to have, but which, unfortunately, could not be obtained locally. And so she had to go. 'Besides,' and here she managed a smile, 'it really is time I saw Foyles.'

But Catherine was a bad liar (for which she had always inwardly complimented herself) and her mother wasn't smiling back. Catherine may have lied with a clear conscience, but she had lied badly and her mother saw it was a lie straight away, and Catherine saw that she saw. She also saw her mother giving her the quick once-over, belly, face and eyes, and Catherine knew what her mother was thinking, or at least the possibility that she was entertaining. Her mother, she felt sure, was remembering the grass stain on her dress the week before and wondering just how long this sort of behaviour had been going on, and equating grass stains with sudden trips to London (for the flimsiest of reasons) and coming up with the inevitable conclusion. Just to set the record straight, for the sake of her own reputation and to sooth her mother's anxieties, she was about to correct what, she felt sure, was the conclusion her mother had reached. But then she stopped herself, for she also realised that to do so would necessitate a conversation that would inevitably lead right back to the very question she wished to avoid: namely, why she was going to London. So she let it be.

To Daniel, a little while later, she simply told the truth – and insisted, upon pain of death (which she would personally administer), that he never tell a soul. Had she read the letter? This was Daniel's immediate question. Of course not! Did she know what was in it? No, she explained, she didn't. Miss Hale had not chosen to tell her – it was, she assumed, personal – and Catherine had not sought to know. It was, Catherine explained, a matter of trust. No, Daniel corrected her, it was a matter of common sense. The letter could say anything and she could, quite conceivably, be drawn into a messy, if not nasty, situation. But that, Catherine replied resolutely, was all part of the trust. She might have mentioned the tobacco tin, the guilt, her subsequent unquestioning acceptance of Miss Hale's request (and that it was all *his* fault, anyway), but didn't.

Now, in the all but deserted high street, Catherine kisses Daniel on the cheek, almost a peck, almost, she notes, in the way that Miss Hale might kiss her friend, or her friend Miss Hale. She has, she says with an apologetic grin, things on her mind, to which Daniel replies that he prefers her when she has only one thing on her mind. With a bigger grin on her face, she leaves, arranging the time and place that they will meet when she returns. And, as she goes, she is pleased to see concern in his eyes – concern that she might have got herself into something just a little over her head. But he also knows that she prides herself on her independent ways, and so he leaves his concern in his eyes where she can read it without need of speech or reply.

Nonetheless, when Catherine falls onto her bed she can't rest, let alone sleep. She can't rest because she knows Daniel is right and she is pronouncing herself a fool for ever agreeing to Miss Hale's request. She doesn't want to go. She'd do just about anything rather than go. And as soon as she fully registers her response to being dragged into something she'd rather have nothing to do with, anger rises up in her. Anger at herself. Anger at Daniel. And yes, anger at Miss Hale for ever asking her in the first place. She, Catherine, would never ask this of anybody, she feels sure. For that would be to take advantage of someone's affections. And one doesn't take advantage of someone's affections because that's how one loses them. But Miss Hale has, and perhaps underlying the whole episode is the assumption on Miss Hale's part that Catherine's affections aren't worth much. And the moment she thinks this, she decides she will not go. Miss Hale can do her own dirty work. Not Catherine. And if Miss Hale doesn't like this, she can go and jump in the nearest river with rocks in her pockets! It is a rotten feeling. Rotten! And the best way to get rid of the rotten feeling is to just not go. It's too much and Miss Hale had no right to ask. But the moment she thinks of not going, she remembers Miss Hale's eyes that morning. She remembers her whole manner – that of a desperate woman who wasn't thinking rationally any more but didn't realise it. Desperate enough to ask a virtual stranger to do this, and, in so doing, open up her most private self to scrutiny. She can't go. She must go. She'll go.

Paddington Station, she notes as she gets off the train the next morning, is not nearly as ugly as everyone has said it is, and does not, as someone famous once said, resemble hell at all. She likes the smoke and the noise and the people. She's put in mind of French impressionist paintings, of stations with exotic names and steam engines and mist. It doesn't exactly look like that, but she's got no doubt that a good painter could make it look like that. But she also knows there's no time for this type of dreamy thinking. There's a job to be done, and the sooner the better.

The signs to the Underground are easy and a holiday mood comes over her. But as she descends, the place takes on a vague resemblance not so much of hell as another world, and a faintly alarming one of shadows and dark figures. You must take the Inner Circle, Catherine. The Inner Circle. Miss Hale's words go round and round in her head as she scans a large map showing her all the lines and all the stations in the city, and, as her fingers follow the line from Paddington to Baker Street, such a short distance, two stops, she smiles faintly at the simplicity of it all. Why do they make such a fuss? Feeling as though she's lived here all her life rather than having just arrived, Catherine heads for her platform.

After a few minutes' wait, she hears the dragon's breath of an approaching train for the first time and feels a sudden and surprising wariness about stepping into and giving herself over to this thing that creates such sounds and travels round in circles all day and night. And the quiet inside, everybody concentrating on newspapers and books, no one catching one another's eyes, adds to the unease and unreality of the journey.

As she steps out of the Underground (both grimy and somehow exciting) and on to the street, the thrill of arriving is overtaken by the thought of the task at hand. And it's the nearness of the place and the task now that confuse her and cause her to walk in the wrong direction. She is walking along a busy street and reaches Madame Tussauds before she realises that Madame Tussauds is not on the map and that she is walking in the wrong direction. So she walks back to the station, losing time, annoyed with herself for getting just a bit too casual and, at the same time, imagining the disappointment of Miss Hale. Once more at the entrance of the station, she realises she was holding the map the wrong way round, and now re-orientates herself and sees clearly where she must go.

A few minutes later when she pauses in front of

the designated flats, a block both high and wide by Catherine's standards, she tells herself that she is simply a messenger. She has a letter to deliver, and a reply to receive. Apart from a brief introduction, she need not even be called upon to talk. And as someone leaves through the front door, she slips into the block and takes the stairs, looking on each level for the number she is after.

When she comes to the flat, her breathing heavy from the climb and a rush of nerves and the residue of the rotten feeling from the night before, she notes that there is a line of light at the bottom of the door, which could be the sun in the room or an inside light. She wavers for a moment, but rather than wait and feel her courage drain she quickly steps forward and knocks on the door. Just get the thing over and done with, she's telling herself. In ten minutes you'll be back on the street. But there is no reply and she knocks again. After a third attempt, she slips the letter under the door, and feels a guilty sense of relief, knowing that her job is now done and that she need not meet the woman, after all. She can, she tells herself, do no more.

But before she reaches the stairs, the door opens and a woman's voice echoes in the landing. And it is not just any voice. She has heard this voice before, if not in fact then in her imagination. And, it is exactly as her imagination told her it would be. This, she knows, straight away, is the voice of the woman who follows her husband about, who is driven to place advertisements in *The Times* calling him home and clings long after she's lost the right to cling. But the recognition of the voice goes deeper than that. This, Catherine knows immediately, is the voice of the woman whose nerves are bad and who threatens at any moment to explode. This is the voice of poetry, poetry Catherine has read again and again, poetry that she has absorbed to the point that she can quote whole passages without even trying. This is that poetry come alive, like a book talking, like a character suddenly stepping out of the page and addressing the startled reader. Startled, and more than a little frightened. For on the page she is simply the product of writing that makes one feel as though she is real, a 'felt experience'. But, standing in front of Catherine, she is, well, uncomfortably *there*. This is that voice, and Catherine is astounded that she knows it so well. As it calls from the door and reverberates around the darkly lit landing, her heart sinks.

'Are you from Tom? Did Tom send you? Did he ask after me? Is he coming?'

It seems to Catherine to be a torrent of questions, all delivered on top of one another at great speed, no pausing in between for full stops or commas. No punctuation. Nothing. Just sheer urgency. Catherine turns to look upon the possessor of the voice that she knows so well but whom she is meeting for the first time, and sees a small, frail-looking woman with eyes that seem to look straight through her with a dangerous, playful innocence, and Catherine's impulse is to run.

But she doesn't. There's nowhere to run. Besides, Miss Hale requires a reply, and for that she must meet this woman who, although small, seems, to Catherine, to be compact and tight, like a spring ready to let fly.

The woman repeats herself. 'Are you from Tom?'

'No-no,' Catherine stammers, amazed that she can talk at all.

'Then what are you doing here? What are you doing knocking on my door? Who *are* you?'

Again this torrent of questions. Catherine has only been in this woman's company for a minute, possibly less, and yet, already, she feels exhausted and drained.

'I was asked,' Catherine says, noting that she sounds infinitely more composed than she feels, 'to bring that letter to you.' And here she points to the envelope that Mrs Eliot is holding (for though Catherine didn't see it, Mrs Eliot must have picked it up when she opened the door).

Mrs Eliot looks down at the letter, almost as if noticing it for the first time, then back to Catherine. 'Who is it from? It's not Tom's hand. I know Tom's hand, and that's not it.'

'It's from a lady.'

'What lady? Why couldn't she bring it herself?'

Catherine simply doesn't know what to say, so she repeats what Miss Hale told her. 'She felt that some things are best said in print.'

'Did she? Then why didn't she just post it? Are we still living in the eighteenth century?'

The questions are relentless, but, Catherine notes, every single one is precise, to the point, and has a logic that is almost impossible to refute. And already, more than simply drained by her company, Catherine feels worn down, worn out. Yes, yes, Catherine might as well say, for she is not sure she has the strength to resist any more. You are quite right, Catherine may as well say, I have no answers. She may be small, this woman, she may have the appearance of being fragile even, but she is all nervous energy and cutting questions, and, all the time, Catherine is reminded of a spring, coiled and ready to let fly.

'Very well, come in,' Mrs Eliot says, more in the manner of a command than an invitation or request.

'Come in?' Catherine hadn't expected this and would rather stay put, anything but step into that flat.

'Yes.' And Mrs Eliot looks her up and down, as if concluding that the girl might be simple. 'Come on. You're not going to stay out here, are you?'

Again, the logic is irrefutable. Of course, it makes absolutely no sense to stand out in the landing while Mrs Eliot goes inside and reads the letter. And so she enters, and Mrs Eliot closes the door behind her, Catherine registering the distant sensation of her heart sinking even further, as well as the distinct smell of … what? Ether?

As they sit, Mrs Eliot fixes her with a direct stare – one of intense scrutiny. 'What's your name?'

'Catherine.'

'Where are you from?'

Catherine knows that this is precisely what she must not tell this woman, that the whole point of delivering the note was to keep this secret: where she comes from, where the letter comes from and so on. It is crucial, she knows this. And so she is vague. 'The country. Up north.'

'Where up north?'

'A small town. You wouldn't know it.'

'Try me. I'm very good on small towns up north.'

Is she making fun of her, or does she always talk like this? Catherine can't decide. 'Broadheath. Near Stretford,' she says.

Catherine did, in fact, once live there, so she can tell her this with some sense of composure. But Mrs Eliot is one of those people who sniff out lies and deception, and Catherine is sure she smells a lie. Mrs Eliot lets it rest however, for she is looking down upon the envelope in her hands. She may be thinking about where Catherine comes from and why she's lying, and she may very well come back to that point later on. But Catherine is not really sure about any of this, for she is distracted. She is both staring at Mrs Eliot and, at the same time, opening her eyes to the overwhelming spectacle of the room in which she is sitting. So much so that she is only vaguely aware of Mrs Eliot ripping at the envelope and unfolding the letter. In front of her, behind her, all around her, it seems on all four walls, are photographs of her husband. From all the phases of his life – young, with the light in his eyes of someone just starting out, the dandy leaning on a brolly and on the brink of fame, to the brooding, mature face of the husband who left on a lecture tour to America in 1932 and never came back. And Mrs Eliot too, from the barely recognisable young woman she was to the one in front of Catherine now. It is impossible not to stare at them all. They demand to be stared at. They are inescapably present. In one that Catherine focuses on directly in front of her, Mr and Mrs Eliot both seem impossibly young. Mrs Eliot, happy, serene even, with none of the shifting edginess in her eyes that she now has, is almost unrecognisable. She is not the same woman. She is clearly vivacious, entrancing, and Catherine knows in an instant why Mr Eliot fell under her spell. They are seated beside each other (either newlyweds, or about to be married, deeply immersed in each other's eyes). Hers are shining – the shining eyes, Catherine notes, of someone gazing upon the object of their adoration and the cause of this look of serene calm she wears. And Mr Eliot, so young he seems to be only just emerging from adolescence, stares back at her with the same longing. But also with what? A sort of trust, Catherine imagines. Yes, trust. As though the world will unfold for him with this young woman, as though with her it will give up its secrets, and with her, he will enter the secret society of grown-up living. Perhaps. Perhaps not. But the more Catherine stares at the photograph, the more she is certain that the young man that was Mr Eliot is handing something over, something he has long wanted to hand over, some part of him – what he might become, his *potential*, yes, that's it – that he entrusts to her. And it is also an admission – that the grandness of his dreams (and his dreams are, indeed, grand) cannot be achieved alone; that he can't do it on his own. And at the bottom of this almost childlike trust in the eyes of the young Mr Eliot is the assumption that she knows more about the ways of the world than he does, and that with her he will be initiated into them. And there is almost a touch of Daniel in that look, and a touch of Catherine in the eyes of the young Mrs Eliot. And she realises with a start that this is a portrait of two young people in love, realises that the man Daniel calls Westminster Abbey on legs was once just a boy with starry eyes. And the woman now reading the letter in front of her, who clings when she has long ago lost the right to cling, once had the dreamy-eyed look of a young woman in love, not a frail woman with that abandoned look all over her face. No, not that. But a young wife, prepared to move heaven and earth for her young man, and confident that she can so that they will both move forward together and live those grand dreams that drive him. And, once again, in the shared dreams and the excitement of setting out in life, she sees in this young couple that Mr and Mrs Eliot once had a hint of Daniel and herself.

There is a sudden humph, then a sigh, and Mrs Eliot turns the page over with audible impatience, once more a coiled spring ready to let fly at any moment, and Catherine is wondering if that moment is now.

The whole room is the same. Photograph upon photograph upon photograph, upon wall upon wall. In one, they are young, punting somewhere or other with friends. In another, Mr Eliot has lost that boyish look, as well as the trust, and Mrs Eliot is no longer a young woman with dreamy eyes but the brittle spring she is now. There are three people in the photograph, and Mrs Eliot is standing apart from the other two, as though she is not wanted and knows it. Mr Eliot is standing beside the long, thin figure of a woman Catherine knows to be the author Virginia Woolf, whom Catherine has never read, but knows one day she will have to. The whole room amounts to a chronicle of the years. A portrait of a marriage. But it's more than that, for as Catherine looks about she concludes that the room is, in fact, a shrine. A place of remembrance. An attempt to freeze time. A place for Mrs Eliot to dwell in and feel as though nothing has changed. Where Mr Eliot might walk in the door at any moment and they would both go on as though nothing had happened. And it is impossible, in this shrine of a room, at this moment, not to see Mrs Eliot as a kind of Miss Havisham, frozen in time. For the room is testimony that she once fell in love, that *they* fell in love, and that words of love and trust once passed between them. Facts, the photographs are pictures of facts, and above all the room is testimony to the fact that the years were hers, his and theirs – and that now, the years having flown, she simply doesn't know how to let them go or what to do with herself. And as Catherine sits there, and as Mrs Eliot huffs and puffs her way through the letter, a treacherous compassion for this woman who clings to all of these things in the room rises in Catherine. For when she calls him her husband, and talks of 'home', as she did in the advertisement, it has the weight of the years documented in these photographs and all the memorabilia contained in the room behind it. And, at the same time, Catherine is also aware of a treacherous shift in her sympathies, and Mrs Eliot no longer frightens and unnerves her as she did just a few moments before. In fact, the very thought of Mrs Eliot had frightened her, such were the images that had inevitably taken root in her imagination after all Miss Hale's talk of her. Such were the images that the poetry created. But now, against all her acquired sense of loyalty, Catherine's heart is going out to this woman who clings, and whose right to do so, she concedes, just might be in the weight of all the years that went before when words of love and trust were surely exchanged between the two of them. And she is dwelling on this when Mrs Eliot slaps the letter down on her knee.

'No!'

Catherine jumps.

'I will not give up my husband. This,' and Mrs Eliot looks up, taking in the room as if drawing life from it, 'this is his home. This is where he belongs, and I will not give him up.'

Catherine says nothing.

'Who is this?' she shrieks, holding the letter up and reading what it says at the bottom. '"A friend of Tom Eliot"? What does that mean? Who sent you? Who *are* you?' With this, Mrs Eliot screws the letter up in both hands and throws it into a wastepaper basket beside her.

Catherine stares at the letter. That is that. Final.

'I assume she – and it *is* a she?'

Again Catherine freezes under her stare and says nothing.

'What does it matter? I assume whoever this "friend" is, whoever this "friend of Tom Eliot" is, he or she will require a reply.' Before Catherine can say anything, Mrs Eliot reaches for writing paper. 'Well, give them this!'

Mrs Eliot scribbles a brief note, reaches for an envelope on the desk, seals it and hands it to Catherine. The writing of the reply, the signing, the sealing, the delivering of the thing to Catherine, is over in a flash. Catherine has Mrs Eliot's letter in her hand.

Mrs Eliot stands. 'Well, I need keep you no longer. Take that back with you.'

Catherine, whose treacherously sympathetic response of just a few minutes before to Mrs Eliot has evaporated, rises, almost jumps to her feet, now only aware of her overwhelming desire to be gone, for there is anger now in Mrs Eliot's eyes and she is looking upon Catherine as one would an intruder. Is this, Catherine is thinking, is this when she springs?

At the door, Mrs Eliot looks her up and down. 'You're the go-between?'

Catherine has never thought of it like this, but she has to admit that, yes, Mrs Eliot is right, she is. But she says nothing.

'They get damaged in the end, don't they?'

A response is clearly not required. Even if Catherine had wanted to reply, there is no time, for Mrs Eliot, not satisfied that she has said all she wishes to say, offers one last comment. 'And you can tell them this. The only true friend Tom Eliot ever had, has or will ever have is his wife. His wife, who sits here every evening, with their dog, the door open, and waits …' And Mrs Eliot nods, as if to suggest that if this is a battle of wills, she will win. She then closes the door, and Catherine is left standing alone on the landing with Mrs Eliot's written reply in her hand, and which she now pushes into her coat pocket.

Back on the street she feels as though she has just stepped out of a cinema. And from a strange, upsetting movie at that. The day is bright, and although the street itself is quiet enough, she is aware of life going on all around her, which she wasn't aware of inside Mrs Eliot's flat. And she is only now conscious of how dull the light was in that room. Not dark, but gloomy. Were the curtains drawn? She can't remember, but the day is bright and the room was dull. Which, along with all the photographs, now makes her feel that the room was not quite part of the world. Not quite part of *this* world, at any rate. And so back on the street she squints and allows time for her eyes to adjust to the light, as she would if she was leaving the cinema. And there are also now the lingering impressions of Mrs Eliot: small (with that odd, puzzling smell of ether, which has left Catherine feeling slightly nauseous), frail looking, even brittle – yes. But she had power, that woman. And Catherine isn't quite sure where that power came from; she only knows that she felt weak in her company. And it wouldn't matter where they met or under what circumstances – if they were to ever meet again, Catherine is sure she would still feel the same. For Mrs Eliot, she sees, is one of those people who have long since given up on social niceties, and who can pin you down with relentless questions and don't give up until you are too tired to resist. And perhaps that explains why Catherine is feeling so drained and exhausted. But it's not just all the questions; it's the way, Catherine suspects, that her heart and her sympathies have been bounced about. She suspects she has a heart that may too easily go out to others. One moment almost physically recoiling from a woman whose very intensity carries a hint of violent impulse, and the next being completely immersed in the shrine of her room, and understanding fully the loneliness that causes her to cling when she has lost all right to. And the fear. That too. For, although Mrs Eliot is, it's true, a frightening woman (for in her presence there was a constant sense of not quite knowing what she would do next, and of Mrs Eliot not knowing herself what she would do next either), she is also, Catherine realises, a frightened woman. Like someone whose life, more or less, has ended. And, who has become a kind of ghost.

Her eyes adjusted now to the brightness of the day, Catherine sets off, up the street, back to the station, to home and to Daniel, whom she suddenly misses with an urgency that surprises her. And the guilt that made her accept Miss Hale's request without pausing to think hangs not so heavily upon her now. Her legs are lighter than they were when she came, and there is a part of her that is tired of this summer game of being one of Miss Hale's girls, a part of her that will be quite happy to see the last of Miss Hale and her special friend.

Early the next morning, as arranged, Catherine meets Miss Hale in her cottage and hands her the reply. Catherine has said nothing of the meeting, has said nothing about her impressions of the woman, and has not let on that she already knows the letter is bad news – that the whole mission, which is what it now seems to have been, was doomed from the outset. And Miss Hale, for her part, has not asked. She is simply eager to open the letter, but, eager as she is, she uses a letter-opener, and is careful not to rip the envelope.

It takes markedly less time to read the letter than to open it, which doesn't surprise Catherine because it took Mrs Eliot virtually no time to write. There is an exasperated sigh; Miss Hale drops the hand holding the letter to her knee, then rises from her chair, placing the letter on a small table, and goes to the window. Catherine has no trouble reading the letter, and she doesn't feel she is snooping, for it seems to have been left face-up on the table for her to view freely. She has, it is implied, earned the right. No wonder it took so little time to write. The message contains five words: 'Never, never, never and never' and is signed, pointedly, 'Mrs Eliot'.

There is a long, long silence, and Catherine is not sure if she can endure the silence without breaking it. But she bites her lip. Then, in a voice almost broken, Miss Hale addresses her. 'What,' and Miss Hale seems to be dragging the question from herself with the utmost reluctance, knowing that it is degrading but not being able to help herself all the same, 'what is she like?'

Catherine's eyes lift from the letter, clear, lit with sudden understanding. This is why she was sent. Not because the letter had to be hand-delivered for the sake of secrecy or discretion or anything remotely like that. She was sent to be the eyes and nose and ears of Miss Hale and come back not only with the reply but with a report of the woman, of what it is like to be in the same room as her; to return with a picture of what it is like to share this woman's company, so that, possibly, Miss Hale could gauge just what it is she is up against. All her explanations had been excuses. *This* is what Miss Hale wants, and what she wanted all along.

With this realisation uppermost in her mind (and she is sure she is right), Catherine allows herself time, while eyeing the back of Miss Hale (the anger of the night before leaving for London rising in her again), to compose her answer so that it says exactly what she wants it to say. For Catherine is one of those who is always thinking after the event of the right thing to say. But not this time.

'She is,' Catherine says, slowly, almost with an actor's air of rehearsed calculation, 'exactly as I imagined – only more so.'

Miss Hale does not turn, but Catherine sees the slightest of nods, weary and resigned, as if to say, 'Yes, that is what I thought, too.' Miss Hale continues to stand at the window for some time, without speaking. She seems, in fact, to have completely forgotten about Catherine. And, as is so often the case in this house, Catherine is not sure if she should stay or go, if her services are no longer required or if something further will be asked of her. But Miss Hale continues to stare out on to the green distance of the garden outside and the countryside beyond. And it is not one of those melodramatic gestures she is prone to. No, Miss Hale is no longer the crying girl; she is simply Miss Hale. She is no longer living, however theatrically, in the world of her youth, but is a middle-aged woman who can no longer pretend that re-entering the world of her youth is a possibility, or that picking up the things of youth from where they were carelessly dropped is a possibility. No, one doesn't simply stride back on stage and pick up the scene (the garden, the two people, the flowers) and bring it all to a satisfactory conclusion with the advantage of hindsight and over twenty years of living to guide it.

For a while during this summer, it must have seemed to Miss Hale that she could have it all back again: her youth, the love she left there but never gave up on, and the young man who eventually became the famous Mr Eliot, but who never ceased to be her Tom. Her whole lost life, seemingly retrieved during one miraculous summer. All through the summer and autumn she had been the crying girl who throws flowers to the ground, who stands at the top of the garden steps and troubles the conscience of her departing lover, and who stays standing there, through the change of seasons, year after year, with reproach in her eyes until the longed-for moment arrives when the lover returns and takes his crying girl in his arms, and everybody is young again and all that was lost is found. And so the scene would conclude. The little play would be over and happiness would be theirs.

But she is no longer the crying girl. She can no longer play the part. She is now simply a middle-aged woman standing at the window, quite possibly about to lose her special friend for the second time, just when she thought that her friend, that long-ago garden and the moment they missed could be theirs again. And it is as she is standing there that the word 'virgin' comes to Catherine's mind. What, Catherine wonders, what must it be to have waited so long, to have kept all of that life bottled up inside her, waiting for that moment in the garden to return so that all that bottled-up life could be released, but to wait in vain all those years? To arrive at one's forty-fourth year and remain the virgin girl who might have loved … What must that be like?

And it is then, as if responding to the unspoken question Catherine has just asked herself, Miss Hale finally turns from the window. 'You can't know, Catherine – you are far too young – you cannot know what it is to lose someone, not once, but twice. But I feel I may.'

For a moment, Catherine wonders if she really did speak when she posed that question to herself. But before she has time to think about it any further, Miss Hale continues. 'We must grasp our moments as they arise, Catherine. And never, never assume that they will come back. People may come back into our lives, but not the time or the moment. And, in the end, not even the people either, for they will be changed. They will not be the same. No,' and here the dreaminess leaves her voice and a sudden urgency enters it, 'no, grasp your moments, Catherine, because they never come back again, and we just spend the rest of our days wishing we'd grasped them when they were there for the taking.'

Miss Hale then falls into silence and Catherine knows that she has given up. Whatever is lost, stays lost. When two people part, they part forever. Even if they come back together, they are not the same people and the life they might have lived is lost forever. And whatever may keep Miss Hale and her friend together or just in touch over the years to come will never be what she came here for this summer and autumn. What she came for was impossible. But this never occurred to her at the beginning of the summer because she was still the crying girl then, frozen in mid-sentence, in mid-gesture, still the crying girl, and still young enough to believe anything was possible.

As Catherine rises, Miss Hale emphasises her point again. 'You must remember that. You won't forget?'

'No.'

She then scrutinises Catherine, almost judging whether this is, in fact, one of those moments. And, concluding that it is (the letter with its four emphatic nevers still spread out on the table), she speaks. 'Your friend – Daniel, yes?'

'Yes.'

'He is leaving soon, is he not?'

'Yes.'

'Tomorrow you come to clean, do you not?'

'Yes.' Catherine nods, mystified, no sense of where this line of questioning might be leading.

'You know that tomorrow the house will be empty. My aunt and uncle will be visiting friends – and I shall be away all day. You know this, don't you?'

'No.' Catherine's eyes widen as the import of what Miss Hale is saying slowly dawns on her.

'Well,' Miss Hale says with a firm nod, 'you do now.'

Catherine looks to the floor, then looks up, not sure what the moment requires.

'Thank you,' she mutters, 'thank you for telling me.'

Miss Hale smiles. 'It's only right you should know. Your duties will be made so much easier, no doubt, for having the house to yourself. And you have the whole day, don't you?'

'Yes.'

'And the whole place to yourself.'

There is a trace of a smile in Miss Hale's eyes, and Catherine returns the look, likewise, with the faintest smile. And in this way an understanding passes between them, and is shared.

It is then that Miss Hale picks up the letter, scrunches it up, and throws the paper ball into the wastepaper basket. Catherine watches it land. A barely discernible thud. As though it had never existed. Miss Hale now wipes her hands, consigning the whole business to the oblivion of the next day's rubbish collection. Catherine finds herself dwelling on the whole business of wastepaper baskets and what ends up in them. Mrs Eliot's letter. Miss Hale's. Both into bins. Both letters, as far as anybody outside the triangle of Miss Hale, Mrs Eliot and Catherine is concerned, never existed. Were never written. The whole episode they have just enacted, the whole nerve-racking mission, never happened.

At the door, Miss Hale thanks Catherine for having undertaken the trip to London. Without saying as much, she implies it is not Catherine's fault that it was all to no avail and that the shadow of that woman will always be hanging over her and her special friend and never let them be. And, once again, she tells Catherine that she has her sincere thanks. But, more than that, Catherine also has her gratitude.

With that, Catherine leaves and steps out into the high street. When she looks back, the door is closed. Miss Hale has retreated, back into the house. Possibly to dwell on those four emphatic nevers, or to remove the wastepaper bin from the room to a place where the letter can be collected and taken from the house altogether, as though, indeed, it never existed.

Outside, the mid-morning street is busy with a mixture of vehicles – old world and new. As she walks back home, Catherine is pondering the curiosity of Miss Hale. For she is a curiosity. Restrained, proper, even prim, but with a whole other life inside her just waiting to burst out, like the gift of French stockings. And so when Miss Hale tells her, with that knowing look, that the house will be vacant the next day, it is both curious and not so curious. For all that life has to burst from her somehow, doesn't it? All those lost moments that were there for the grasping at the time, but which never were because of an assumption that time goes on and on, cry out to be lived somehow. Don't they?

When Daniel leaves, he may do so for good, or he may return as he swears he will. He may, indeed. But Catherine knows, and she bravely tells herself, that they are young, with whole lives to be lived that may or may not include each other. They may never have a life together at all, but they will (and Catherine's mind is dwelling on the image of Miss Hale at the window, forever at the window, her voice almost broken) have their moment. They will have this much. And in the bustle of the street Catherine is aware of moments, greetings and cheerios, the opening and closing of a shop door, a farming cart and the clip-clop of a horse mingling with the engine sounds of a passing motor car. Moments gathered together, strands of the day's music tapering into the long, drawn-out hum of the car as it leaves the town. They may not have a life together but they will have the days. And that, she tells herself, is how a life is lived, through moments and through days.

The sun glints on the rooftops along the street. The windows sparkle. Her feet move swiftly. Daniel will, at this minute, be in his father's shop, and she moves towards it with urgency in her step, for she has not spoken to him since returning from London and there is much to tell.

PART FOUR

Intercession
Late September, 1934

Was it an accident that she came home early, or did she do so on purpose? Or did she do it, as the phrase would have it, 'accidentally on purpose'? Whatever, she is back. And she is early.

The house has been cleaned. Everything spotless. Everything exactly where it ought to be. Everything is in order, in its place. A model of how the universe ought to be. And quiet. The kind of quiet that a house has when nobody is home. And Emily Hale assumes that nobody is.

It is mid-afternoon. The day is still and sunny, with the hint of a chill. She has been to see a country house nearby, but there are only so many gardens and houses that you can admire before your attention starts to wander. And besides, she was alone (apart from the owner who kindly allowed the visit), and these things are best seen with a friend, preferably a special friend. It is then the flowers glow and the lawns sparkle. But she was alone, and not wearing a watch had lost track of time, and weary of gardens and lawns and old estate houses she excused herself and strolled back along a well-trodden walking track that took her back into town. And she felt quite the native returning in this manner. No, she didn't need a lift, she'd told the owner, and no, she didn't need directions home – all of which impressed him. Yes, she felt quite the native. The sheep bleated and the cows looked up from time to time from their munching, and she felt at home. Except she wasn't. And she knew she wasn't. Her friend, for whom she'd crossed land and sea and time, was in London, at work. She was in the country, and bored with country houses, with their estates and gardens. Would this be the way of things? She, always the woman who must be tucked away in some quaint country town in a foreign country, waiting on visits from her friend, who must not say a word of her except to those to whom he is close enough to confide in? And even those friends close enough to confide in, she was sure, no matter how much their loyalties would always be with her friend, would always see her as his stuffy Boston lady. Stuffy, over-refined. Like one of those women from Mr James whose observations always bear the imprint of a provincial intelligence. One look at the long, bony nose and beady eyes of Mrs Woolf and she was convinced that this was exactly what she thought of her. The whole bunch of them for that matter. She, Miss Hale, forever judged and forever found wanting; refined, polite and dull, only ever tolerated – perhaps indulged, at best – because she was Tom's special friend, and, therefore, *must* be tolerated. It was no way to live, and who were they to judge, anyway? And how could anybody put up with those eyes and those silences that would inevitably follow anything she said in conversation, unless, of course, her friend came to her rescue. Which would set everybody off, and then they'd all be talking. The conversation would continue. She would be forgotten. She, the stuffy Boston lady, forever tucked away in some quaint little town … It was only at this point that she'd realised that she was clutching a handful of crisp autumn leaves and a brown stem that she must have snatched from a bush along the way. She'd compressed them in her fist to such a degree that the leaves were crushed and the stem had dug into her palm (or perhaps this had happened when she snatched the leaves from the bush), leaving a small cut with a red smudge around it. Only then did she feel the sting. She'd stopped, and looking down at her palm and the blood asked herself when this ridiculous business had started. *Is* this, indeed, the way it would always be? As much as she might have commended herself on being quite the native when she left the estate she'd just visited, walking back to town was another matter. Thoughts about the way things would be, about the pattern that was emerging, had made her ratty (not a word she often used) and restless – and, yes, *far* from home.

Besides, as much as she tried to ignore them, thoughts of Catherine surfaced at odd moments during the day. Catherine and this young man of hers. Now back in the house and finding it still and quiet, she assumes, and is relieved to assume, that it has simply been cleaned, tidied and left. She assumes that the house has been arranged and left undisturbed for much of the day. Her aunt and uncle are, presumably, still away visiting friends, and although she contemplates calling out just to see if they might be in, she sees no need. After the ratty and irritable finish to the day, she needs peace and rest.

When she goes upstairs and takes the connecting door through to her cottage, she is aware of the soothing quiet of the place and is thankful for it. Distant, occasional birdsongs from the high street outside the window filter through into the ordered tranquil rooms. But nothing much more.

It is only as she is about to drop her cardigan onto the chaise longue under the window in her bedroom that she hears something that doesn't belong. And at first she doesn't recognise the sound, only that it doesn't fit in with the neatness and calmness of the place and that it is an intrusion. But what? Then it returns, louder this time, and she knows right away that this sound is coming from the small bedroom next to hers, just on the other side of the stairs that lead down to the lounge room of the cottage. It is muffled but quite audible, the sound of someone groaning, or gasping, the way one does when experiencing deep pain, or, perhaps, deep pleasure. And instantly, as she quietly sinks onto the chaise longue, she knows who is behind that door, no more than ten or twelve feet from where she is sitting.

And, as much as a voice says don't listen, as much as a voice says don't stay, just rise and leave as quietly as you came, she stays, and the sound draws her in. And the more she listens, the louder it becomes, whether it is because she is listening more intently or because it is louder and because that small second bedroom (which may, at some stage, have been a maid's room) is *so* close, she doesn't know. But it grows and grows in volume. Until it fills the air and it is as though some dreadful act of violence is taking place in the next room. Murder. Strangulation. Heaven knows what. Then it comes again, louder still. And, as much as she wants to be gone now, as much as she simply does not wish to hear any more, and as much as she now feels an intruder in her own house, and as much as a voice inside her tells her that such sounds are beneath the lady, she stays, for she is in the sound's thrall. This thing, this thing that is going on in the next room, has her in its thrall, and as much as the angel of her better nature counsels her to go, the beast of temptation holds sway, and she knows as she sinks further into the long chair that the lady has made her choice. And the sound seems to grow even more, if that is possible. It is a woman, or was once a woman. For this young woman, Catherine, is making old, old sounds, sounds that existed long before houses and estates and trimmed rose gardens. Long before sweet music, stained-glass windows that glow with a touch of heaven, or even fine, uplifting words that allow us to rise above it all, for it is a sound that goes back beyond words. It is a sound that takes her back to the age of the grunt and the moan. And this is what draws her in – as the elevated *will*, with longing and disgust, look upon the animal they imagine they once were. This is what has her in its thrall, this sound of the thing itself taking place in the next room. This is it. The wordless swamp to which lovers go. But, even as she utters the word 'swamp' to herself, the shudder that passes down her spine also carries with it the thrill of a shiver. This is the thing that takes young couples out to the sheep paddocks where only the animals can hear and look upon them. This is the thing that announces itself through the grass stains on the skirts of young women strolling back hand in hand from the paddocks with the young men who led them there or whom they led.

Then, there is a louder gasp, a gasp of pain, surely. For she felt it. She felt it as surely as if she were in that room, the room where, right now, two people are entering that world of shared knowledge and experience that she has never entered and which she knows she never will. There are, she has told Catherine often enough, different kinds of love, and Miss Hale and her friend have chosen theirs. And she asks herself once more: was it an accident that she came home early or was it on purpose? Or did she do it 'accidentally on purpose'? And did she seek to brush with this knowledge and experience that is open to any local girl, and which she might readily find in a sheep paddock on any summer evening, but which will never be hers because it must now remain beneath the lady and beneath her friend? And, because of this, did she come back to hear the sound of knowledge being acquired and exchanged? And just as she submits herself to this relentless questioning, telling herself not to be shocked (from the moment she sank into the chaise longue she knew that all shock was mere pretence, for she had come here to be shocked), just as she was telling herself not to be revolted because she had come here to be revolted, and just as she was telling herself not to pronounce any of this beneath the lady (for the lady had come to fall), there is an extended gasping sound, the kind of gasp that is emitted when someone is hit by a pain so sudden it takes their breath away, and her brain stops. Her brain is numbed, as if having *felt* the experience along with Catherine. And the sound goes on and on, seemingly without end, a sound that is beyond caring who or what hears, a sound that may as well be coming from a sheep paddock as a room. And Emily Hale *is* there. She, too, is emitting it, this sound that doesn't care who hears because it comes from so long ago – before music, manners and fine words. And when it fades, when the sound subsides, Emily Hale, too, physically feels her body collapse with the dying fall of the sound in the next room, feels her back, stomach, legs and chest sigh into welcome rest. Her head drops, the imagined pain lessens, and she listens.

Her ears strain, but there is nothing. Only silence. A deep, almost lush silence. A restful silence, she imagines. The silence that, well, lovers fall into when they have finished their love-making. The moment of languid ease that paintings of lovers choose to depict, the moment after the brutality of the love-making is over and done with. This is that silence. The silence that poems and novels give you, when you know something momentous has taken place, when two people, two halves have come together briefly, and rest separately afterwards. No, not separately. Possibly they are holding hands. Perhaps they are still locked in embrace. She can only imagine the scene in the room. And she dwells on the many possibilities, for the quiet calm that hangs in the air is the kind of calm that calls forth contemplation and speculation. And even though she is shaken throughout her whole body, she remains perfectly still, albeit sunk, into the chaise longue, her thoughts floating on the now calm air. She could almost doze off into restful sleep herself. And so she stays in the thrall of this all too welcoming silence much longer than she knows she really ought to. But as much as a distant voice tells her that she has stayed too long, and dwelt much too long in its thrall, she stays on. And on, taking it all into her.

But at some point it also occurs to her that it is an unnerving silence, one which, it strikes her, is even more frightening than the sounds she has just borne witness to. More frightening because the silence – and there is now something unnatural about it – cuts her off, excludes her from the thing taking place in the next room. Until now she had heard the gasps, and felt the rest. Until this silence, that is, which has cut her off from the thing and rendered whatever is now going on in that room an utterly private experience as apart from a 'felt' one. But of course she knows she felt nothing and emitted no sounds, only imagined pain and imagined pleasure. She no more felt any of it than she would a printed kiss. She no more felt any of it than she would the softness and moist warmth of written lips. And somehow, at this moment, that's not enough. And as she lifts her head and takes in the pervasive silence, which has now returned to the house, she is feeling what she at first takes to be envy. Envy that this young girl, who is the same age that she was when she stood in that long-ago Boston garden, has taken this knowledge into her, and that all she, Emily Hale, will ever know of it is the sound of knowledge being acquired and becoming experience.

But slowly, in the continuing quiet, something different, reassuring, almost comforting, comes to her. For when she tries to imagine herself where this young Catherine now is, and the sweet, smiling face of her special friend where this young Daniel is, she can't. It would destroy them. She knows this. It is impossible. No, after these last few minutes (or were they more – she has lost all track of time?) she cannot now imagine herself in that room, and perhaps she has never been able to imagine herself like this. What we become is what we are, and what we were always going to be. And what she was back there in that long-ago Boston garden is what she is now. So when she imagines herself in their place she can't. Or won't. They are, presumably, naked. Visible to each, completely naked … no, it is impossible. She cannot conceive of herself naked before her friend, or he suffering the indignity of being naked before her. It would destroy them. It is beneath her, but, more importantly, beneath *him*. No, she could never conceive of herself in that room (and she is relieved that Catherine has chosen the spare room with its single, maid's bed and not hers, otherwise she could never sleep in her own bed again) where love of a certain brute kind has just been exchanged. She could never conceive of it, and nor could her friend. And if the accident of returning early has taught her anything, it has taught her this.

But while she is absorbing all of this, she is also aware that this silence, this sleep into which the house has fallen, presents another problem. The problem of leaving without being heard. For her footsteps, the opening and closing of the door that leads back into the house, will surely be amplified in the silence. But, at the same time, she knows she must leave, and that she must not forget her cardigan, for it will show Catherine that she has been here and heard everything. But, as she is reaching for it, as she is about to make her exit, the door of the next room (which is directly opposite the chaise longue and of which she has a clear view because *her* door is open) bursts open with an eruption of laughter.

Daniel, like some indolent child of the aristocracy, has just, in the manner of dismissing the staff, ordered the 'maid' back to work. But Catherine has no sooner burst into laughter than she opens the door and the laughter stops. She thinks she must have imagined it. That her guilt has conjured up Miss Hale. But she's not a vision, a product of the imagination, guilty or otherwise. It's her, all right. And she's just sitting there, on the other side of the stairwell, under her wide bedroom window, on the … what do you call it? … chaise longue, directly in front of her, no more than ten or twelve feet away, as surprised at the sudden appearance of Catherine as Catherine is surprised at the sudden materialising of Miss Hale.

One look in her eyes and Catherine (who has mercifully remembered to throw on her loose everyday working dress) is convinced she has made a dreadful mistake. That she has completely misunderstood everything. That Miss Hale informed her of certain facts about the house being vacant the day before purely in the line of duty, things that she, as casual domestic staff in the service of Miss Hale, ought to know, and that was that. But she, Catherine, hadn't left it at that, had she? Catherine had concluded from all this exactly what she wanted to conclude, and, in the process, had got things dreadfully wrong. One look at Miss Hale's eyes, and she is convinced of this. These are Miss Hale's rooms, after all. But she has had the presumption to treat them as her own. Like those servants in romping stories that get up to all sorts of high-jinks when the master's away, but who are inevitably found out, and in the most flagrantly compromised manner. How could she? How could she get it so wrong? These are Miss Hale's rooms and she has soiled them, as surely as she has soiled the sheets. What on earth had she been thinking?

Catherine stands stock still in the doorway. Daniel, thank goodness out of view, lying naked on the tiny single bed and having heard the guillotine come down on Catherine's laughter, has immediately concluded that the lady is back. Absurdly, but reflexively, he pulls a sheet over him (which Catherine catches from the corner of her eye, and which almost, against her will, causes her to burst into yet more laughter), and turns his face, frozen in apprehension, to the doorway and to Catherine. They are two children caught out while up to no good – or caught out in the execution of some prank they have mutually agreed upon. They are suddenly aware of their nakedness. Expelled from the brief paradise of having a room of their own. Catherine, motionless in the doorway, everything, arms, legs, hands, perfectly still (as if she were modelling the scene), staring directly back at Miss Hale.

It is, Catherine imagines, like one of those childish games when two people stare at each other and the first to blink loses. And she is convinced it will be her because she is so clearly in the wrong for having taken advantage of Miss Hale's rooms in the most unforgivable way, for having broken her trust so completely. And she is about to drop her chin to her chest and find some words to say, although she is not sure she can speak at all at the moment. But, unbelievably, it is Miss Hale who breaks first. Miss Hale who blinks, whose gaze shifts down to the floor. An odd gesture of what? Of dismissal, that she can't bear to look upon her any more? That the very sight of Catherine is distasteful? It might be, but something in the way her body slumps tells Catherine that it is not distaste or dismissal. Something in the lady's slumped posture tells her otherwise. And she doesn't need to think too long on what this lowering of the eyes means. For, Catherine is thinking, haven't we all done precisely this? Haven't we all lowered our eyes in admission … of what? Of guilt? Yes, that's it. Haven't we all done this? Yes, yes. Only Catherine had never thought she'd see the eyes of Miss Hale lowered in such a manner. But this is precisely what has just occurred, and in Miss Hale's gesture Catherine reads apology. And in reading apology she also reads that permission was always granted, and that she hadn't got things dreadfully wrong. That she hadn't soiled Miss Hale's rooms as surely as she had soiled the sheets. That Miss Hale is not the sort who just comes out and says things, and that Catherine had understood her instructions perfectly.

An odd sense of power accompanies the realisation. And, once more, the word 'virgin' occurs to Catherine as she contemplates the slumped figure of Miss Hale in front of her. Miss Hale, who has loomed larger than life through her summer, but who now has never looked so small. Again, the word 'virgin' comes to her. And this is where her sudden sense of power comes from, for Catherine holds in her hands the testimony (a rolled-up bed sheet with a visible small red smudge) that she, Catherine, has had the experience – whether it brought pleasure or was simply something to be endured in the end, for the pleasure and the pain are not the point – she, Catherine, has had the experience that has haunted Miss Hale all these years. Something Miss Hale has sought out, in one way or another, all these years. Not just the act, but the completion of a moment left suspended. And for a while it must have seemed that ordinary love (and it was perhaps the ordinariness that would have been bestowed upon her, not the act itself, that mattered) might have come Miss Hale's way. But it wasn't to be. No, her friend, instead, had bestowed upon her a 'different' kind of love.

As she is staring at Miss Hale, who has not yet looked up, an entirely new thought occurs to Catherine. And she is almost as stunned by the thought as she was by the sudden appearance of Miss Hale. That whole sense of entering a story, if only vague or occasionally nagging, but which has, nonetheless, persisted all summer, rises in her. And while standing there, with Daniel's expectant face just visible from the corner of her eye, Catherine silently addresses Miss Hale, with the clear insight and the concentrated wisdom of her eighteen-and-a-half-year-old mind. Is this it, she is silently asking? Is this the life you never had, the one you might have had all those years ago? Oh, you might not even have been aware of it but is this what you wanted, and is *this* what we had to give each other all along: a 'felt experience'?

And now it's not Catherine who feels as though she has intruded upon Miss Hale. For, in this moment in which wild thoughts and feelings tumble over one another, and which she knows will stay with her forever in relentlessly detailed clarity, she is asking herself just how long Miss Hale has been there? And how much of that private world of Catherine and Daniel's has been heard, listened in on, and, thereby, made public? For, just one pair of ears, one listener, one eavesdropper (however intentional or unintentional) is enough to turn a private moment into a public one. Or, even a performance. So, far from being the one who has intruded, Catherine is now feeling intruded upon. And, however consciously or unconsciously determined, there is the nagging thought in Catherine's mind that she has delivered, on cue, the right scene at just the right moment.

All of this, from laughing at Daniel's feigned aristocratic indolence, to locking eyes with Miss Hale and witnessing the lowering of her gaze, has taken a matter of seconds – ten, possibly fifteen. She is not sure, for it is one of those moments in which you are not aware of minutes and seconds, not the usual moments that fill your days. They're special ones that say to you you're going to remember this – in every minute detail. But as she snaps out of the spell, and while Miss Hale's head is still bowed, Catherine becomes conscious of the bundle she bears, with the small red smudge visible at the top, and wonders what to do with it. And it is only then that she remembers where she was going before she came face to face with Miss Hale when she opened the door. And, as any cleaning maid would, she does what Daniel in all his feigned indolence ordered her to do. She returns to work, assuming the manner of the domestic staff she is, and walks straight down the stairs, leaving behind the bowed figure of Miss Hale without speaking, taking the soiled sheet to the laundry to be cleaned. And, as she strides away, out into the open sunshine of the common garden at the back where the laundry is, she knows, beyond doubt, that Miss Hale will be gone by the time she returns. And that then she and Daniel can leave their room, leave the house (unoccupied as promised) and merge back into the street life of the postcard town, which will be Daniel's for only a few days more and which Catherine cannot, now, wait to be shot of.

Control. Power. And yes, a certain satisfaction accompanies the whole action. But, as she enters the back garden, there is something else. A quickening of the heart. A fluttering of the nerves. A sense of having, intuitively, stepped into a role and triumphed. And, in the process, of having *lived* with an intensity that makes her hunger for more and leaves her tingling all over.

A week later, Catherine watches the bus containing Daniel lumbering up the high street of the town. She is, she knows, watching him leave. And he is waving to her through the rear window of the bus, his face sad in a way that she can't quite define. She is not reflective at this moment; she is barely even thinking. She is only conscious of something being wrenched from her. A painful wrenching. Of course, she's had all this time to prepare herself. But not only is Daniel being wrenched from her, so is the 'us', the 'we', the 'them' that had spent the summer together. When did she start talking like that? When did she start making plans in the plural? She has no idea, for it happened without her noticing. But one day this summer she started thinking in terms of 'us' and 'we', and it is only now that she realises how much it had meant – to be two. And the sadness hasn't even hit her yet. It's too soon for sadness. For the moment there is only this wrenching feeling. As well as that odd, puzzling sensation that it can't be real, it can't be true. She's not *really* standing in the street waving goodbye to a bus taking Daniel from her. Possibly forever. Other people say goodbye, other people leave each other, not Catherine and Daniel. Then she reminds herself that he will come back and that they will be writing to each other all the time he is away. It is not goodbye, but *au revoir*. And with that little French thought, a flicker of a smile lights her eyes. All the same, she's glad she's back at school. Glad the tasks of her final year will swamp her mind, numb her feelings and fill her days with work. Perhaps, if she's lucky, the year will be over before she knows it.

The bus recedes, the same bus that they have so often taken to the cinema at the towns nearby, or just for the sake of an afternoon trip. But this, she tells herself, as his face becomes smaller and smaller, is no afternoon trip. And, in the years to come, she will realise that beneath the pain of losing Daniel, the Catherine who is standing back and watching at this moment knew perfectly well all along that something final was taking place. And that, just then, what she saw in Daniel's eyes as he stared back at her through the rear window of the bus was the admission that this was goodbye, not *au revoir*. And the sadness of the moment is this: that for all his talk he is, in fact, seeing his Catherine for the last time through the eyes of someone in love. But they don't know this yet. And though they will meet again, they will never look upon each other with love in their eyes as they have this summer.

And no matter how much he swears he's coming back for her, he won't. And as much as he swears that he will miss her, there will come a day when he won't. And she won't. And they will both know that what they have just shared is what books, and the world for that matter, call first love. And just as books and plays very sensibly leave the story of first love at the climactic moment, so will Catherine and Daniel.

Then the bus is gone, around the corner at the top of the high street, and with it the last of Daniel. And as she turns to go, the sensation comes back again, that wrenching feeling.

And Miss Hale? Catherine has glimpsed her in the street once since the week before, for being back at school she no longer has time for cleaning. The distance was sufficient for them both to ignore each other. She went on her way (to the baker, the butcher, she can't remember) as though she had never made the acquaintance of the refined Boston lady, or her special friend, and had never received the privilege of being counted as one of Miss Hale's girls. And Miss Hale went her way as if Catherine could have been just anybody – one of the local girls who got up to all sorts of things in summer fields at nights.

A high, singing note soars above Catherine's head, hovers there, then joins with others and becomes a tumbling, descending rush of music, falling on her, for the music that she and Daniel first heard in the lunchtime concert at the local church has become the music of the summer, their summer song, and she feels it fall on her now as she leaves the bus stop behind, leaves behind the house in the high street that introduced her to Miss Hale, her special friend, the woman who clings long after she has lost the right to do so and that whole storybook world that came with them all. And that something else, that secret thrill of having delivered into the world a 'felt experience', precisely on cue, the right gesture at exactly the right time.

As she leaves behind the street, the shops, the houses of the town and wanders down the lane that only a few weeks before she and Daniel had found so conveniently deserted, she takes with her the sadness of Daniel's departure and the curious sense of triumph and power that comes with doing other people's living for them.

PART FIVE

The Rose Garden

1990s

A string quartet is setting up on the lawns. It is mid-afternoon and the autumn sun is still warm. The guests, all in their formal party clothes, are chatting quietly while a cellist tunes her instrument. Gusts of laughter and the shouts of children disturb the uniform murmur of the crowd from time to time. It is an inviting scene, but Catherine has slipped away for a few minutes. She looks back over her shoulder as she crosses the lawn. Everyone is still locked in chat. Her cousin's husband is intent on mastering the complexities of his new camera while his grand-daughter, in her white gown, is contemplating his confusion with a slow shake of the head. No one looks up. Good. No one has noticed that Aunt Catherine has given them the slip for a few moments.

When she reaches the rose garden, Catherine stops. The effect of being here again is stronger than she expects. Or is it that, knowing it to be an occasion of some moment, she has stopped dead in her tracks because she feels she ought to stop – in deference to the occasion? Going back is always like that, she thinks; are we really moved, or do we merely think we *ought* to be moved, and therefore are? After a lifetime of manufacturing other people's feelings on cue, she is a little sceptical of her own. Nonetheless, when she stops at the border of the rose garden she is moved, even if there is a faint element of performance in the moment.

Fifty years ago? Even more than that. Was it really? To Catherine, peering down upon the scene for only the second time in her life, nothing, neither the garden nor the house, has changed, just the world outside.

Behind her, a giant marquee has been set up on the front lawns of the house and a wedding reception is in progress. A marriage has taken place, just a few hours before in the town's parish church; her cousin's grand-daughter, at the age of eighteen, has impetuously married a young man in his early twenties. Everybody told them, everybody warned them: don't do it, they said. But of course they did it. Catherine turns, and her eyes rest for a moment on this young woman, now demonstrating the workings of the camera to her grandfather. Catherine, who, without any lasting regret, has no children of her own, looks upon this young woman as a kind of grand-daughter and there is a touch of the maternal in her gaze. Just then the bride looks up and sees the solitary figure of her 'aunt' on the edge of the estate lawns. They smile at each other. Even from this distance, Catherine sees the light of life in her eyes, and as she does the word 'ardent' occurs to her. 'Ardent,' she hums, is their word – this ardent young woman and ardent young man; together they have acted upon their ardent impulses and done this impetuous thing. The moment is theirs, she thinks, and whatever may follow – boredom, divorce or everlasting happiness – no one can take this moment from them now.

The smile is still in her eyes as she steps into the garden, roses pink and white glowing in the still light of the afternoon. The flowers, the drained pools, the house and sky that hangs above them all, untouched by the years. Dictators have tumbled (Herr Hitler won and lost his Rhineland), war has destroyed whole cities and murdered millions, the moon has been deflowered and the computer has been born.

But none of these things, or so much more that the years have brought, are in evidence here. And as she strolls up the central path, the rose stems inclining towards her like old friends welcoming her back into their timeless midst, the phrase 'pathetic fallacy' interrupts her thoughts. For as much as she tells herself that flowers are just flowers, she has been, nonetheless, mentally bowing to the roses and the roses have bowed back. A short conversation, enquiries about her welfare after all this time, where she has been and what she has seen are surely not far away.

And it is then, while she is lost in a world of memory and speculation, that she hears it. Laughter. The bushes behind her are laughing. She swings around. Did she really bow to the flowers? Did she talk to the roses, and is the shrubbery behind her now shaking with laughter? As she peers into the shady green leaves, two young children burst from the bushes, their laughter trailing behind them as they speed across the open lawn to the marquee. And she has no sooner registered their laughter than she has turned back to the shrubbery, now still. For she knows this spot, and the two young people it once concealed in another age, a time people now call 'between the wars', although nobody ever thought of it like that then. The eighteen-year-old Catherine and the twenty-two-year-old Daniel. They're not here to be seen now, only the shrubbery and the low-hanging branches that once hid them, and from which Daniel's laughter, too, once irreverently rose. And because they are not here to be seen, and only the shrubbery is, she feels the moment more. For this is the way it will be. This is the way it will always be. Disregarding the possibilities of fires and bombs and whatnot, earth, buildings and trees will all go on, while she, and everyone with whom she's crossed paths, will not. Like Daniel.

They did see each other again. Briefly, for a week, when he came to see her on a short trip from Paris. But it wasn't the same Daniel, not the same Catherine, not the same 'them'. As much as he told her he was in love, his love did not travel with him. Nor did hers stand still and wait. And as much as they tried to pick up where they'd left off, they couldn't. They'd grown, and grown apart. Foolish to think they could ever pick things up. That last glimpse she'd had of him, as he looked back to her from the rear window of the bus when he left the town to live in Paris, was the last time they looked at each other through the eyes of two young people in love. And, perhaps, she'd known it all the time. Amid the sadness of things ending, of the summer being finally over, she had known that this was the way it was always going to be. That they'd given each other all they were ever going to give. His letters would come in, and her letters would go out to him. But one day, in their heart of hearts, they had known that the letters would stop. Perhaps she had known that the pain of having Daniel wrenched from her would fade, become a memory, and they would very sensibly just get on with things.

It wasn't until years later that she learned from a friend who'd taught briefly with him that he married and slipped back into the country without ever telling her. And why not? What was there to say? That 'ardent' was their word, but that he'd wearied of their ardent ways? And that thing he was groping towards, that way of thinking about the world he'd talked about often enough but could never quite describe, yet felt sure he would find over there? Perhaps he did find it. In the mid-sixties, her mother, who was retired but liked, as she put it, to keep 'in touch', showed her an article in a literary quarterly by an academic at Birmingham with Daniel's name.

It was, she'd said, an article about the new Citroën. You know, the car! A *serious* article. And Catherine remembered her mother shaking her head, not so much puzzled as disbelieving of this new world of 'theories'. She couldn't understand a word of it, she said, and what she did she didn't like, but she thought Catherine might be interested. They were, apparently, a 'school', this Birmingham crowd, and that gave her mother a laugh. 'Like fish.' And she'd opened and closed her mouth as she'd laughed.

Catherine thought about Daniel more often, she imagined, than he ever thought about her, and was always happy that he seemed to have found that thing he was groping towards but could never see clearly enough to define. And although she'd sobbed and moaned when the letters stopped, and although she knew that they'd stopped because he'd met someone else, she'd also recognised that it was as it should be. They'd lived inside a golden circle but could never step outside. And, once they did, for the world in which the rest of their lives would be lived was always calling, they had to leave it all behind, their ardent ways and those golden circle days when 'ardent' was their word. And the difference in the lives they had lived since then only served to confirm this. He, the academic, the teacher he swore he would never become, settled, apparently happy, in the same city (not far from where he grew up) all his life. His life (job, wife, three children and seven grandchildren), one, it seemed, of contented routine, no doubt punctuated by the odd prank.

He, all of this, and she the shiftless one. For when Catherine finished her final year of school, she did earn a scholarship to university (Manchester, not Cambridge), where she not only discovered acting but discovered that she was very good at it. Discovered that she not only had a natural gift for delivering a 'felt experience' on cue (a director's dream) but delighted in the experience. Thrilled inwardly every time she felt the audience living, through her and her alone, one of those lives they would never live, but the experience of which she could give them for a few transcendent moments. And once she knew she had the gift, she nursed and nurtured it every year of her life. As she still does. For 'Aunt' Catherine is famous. Famous for the many gutsy women she has brought to life on stage and screen, for the many romantic and suggestive scenes she has had no qualms about doing and which, surprisingly, her mother took in her stride. And famous for her political views, which, one evening on television, saw her going head to head with Mrs Thatcher and coming out rather well. And, even then, she could feel half the country surging behind her as she gave them a 'felt' political experience they'd so longed to have. So when she knew she had the gift of delivering such experiences, she nurtured it. What better way to give people all those lives they'd never live, those lives we inevitably lose in living?

And throughout her life (two marriages, a trail of boyfriends and lovers), throughout her career (famous for her outspoken beliefs about *living* life's moments as they arise, the actress Daniel must surely have seen sometime, who'd lived much of her life both home and abroad), she never lost the memory of that first performance and her first audience, never forgot the eyes of Miss Hale in the bedroom of her cottage as they stared back at her, that unmistakable mixture of gratitude and shame written all over her face, never forgot the exhausted way Miss Hale's body had slumped and her head had lowered, as though having finally experienced the very thing she had both dreaded and longed for all her life. And it was Catherine who'd given it to her.

But even though there was a mixture of gratitude and shame written across Miss Hale's features that afternoon all those years ago, Catherine concluded that she'd chosen to disown the thing that Catherine had given her and for which she'd so longed – disowned it as being 'beneath' the lady. And after that day, the two women had never spoken again.

That was the end of Miss Hale, or it would have been had Catherine not, in the mid-seventies, picked up a critical study of Mr Eliot at a second-hand bookshop one Sunday afternoon. She'd flicked through the book in her car and come to a stop at a section entitled 'Burnt Norton'. She, of course, knew the poem, had never ceased reading Mr Eliot, and he had never ceased to be *her* poet. She didn't feel the need of other people's opinions (since they were bound to get it wrong), and so rarely read the critics or biographers. But this was one of those never-ending Sundays and she'd picked up the book with eager relief. And when she came to the section entitled 'Burnt Norton', she noted there was also a photograph of the house, of the drained pools and the rose garden, and she mentally occupied her place in the foliage, sighed all over again for Miss Hale, and urged her on to happiness as if it were still a possibility. At the same time she noted that the critic, apparently a learned Eliot scholar, had written that there was nothing personal in the choice of location for the poem. Catherine gave a brief smile. She had never, over the years, let on to anybody about Miss Hale and the events of that summer and autumn. They were personal, and entailed confidences and trusts that could never be broken. In this respect, Catherine had remained one of Miss Hale's girls all of her life. She had received Miss Hale's trust, and she would never betray it. Let them write what they will. Catherine was there; she knew otherwise, knew the power and significance of unrecorded events that may as well never have existed, and letters that end up in wastepaper baskets and that may as well never have been written. There was also a superstitious part of Catherine that entertained the idea that a betrayal of trust somehow bestowed a curse upon the betrayer. She, who in her youth had scoffed at the idea of Mr Eliot and his Furies, was now wary of them.

There was a brief footnote on the page that suggested Mr Eliot may have visited the house with a friend. Miss Hale's name was not mentioned. She had become the footnote that she must have always feared she would become. The crying girl who may as well never have existed, whose essence ends up stoppered in a small bottle, whose name may or may not be remembered depending on the whims and interests of those who uncork the bottle. In the seventies and eighties, however, the nameless footnote was finally named, and a number of biographers 'discovered' Miss Hale. And there was speculation as to the importance of Miss Hale: was she the muse in the rose garden? Or was she simply an old friend who was merely coincident with the moment? Who really knew? Throughout it all, Catherine kept her confidences.

Somehow, and she couldn't remember how, Catherine discovered that Miss Hale died alone in 1969, three years after Mr Eliot's death, in Massachusetts. Miss Hale would have read in the papers, as indeed Catherine had, about Mr Eliot's marriage to his secretary in 1957, would have subsequently learned about the happiness of the marriage, and Catherine could only wonder what she thought whenever she spoke of it or was asked. For Catherine is convinced that she would never have uttered her real thoughts for fear that they may have been considered 'beneath' the lady.

It was about the same time that Catherine heard

of Mrs Eliot, dead in an asylum in London years before, protesting her sanity till the end, although she apparently had few visitors to protest it to; probably still in love, still waiting for Mr T.S. Eliot to return to 68 Clarence Gate Gardens. But all Catherine could remember were the walls of her flat, photograph after photograph, documenting her life with Mr T.S. Eliot, with Tom, photographs with her, preserved forever, as his 'true companion'. And the faint whiff of ether, and the voice, the voice that Catherine knew already before she even heard it all those years ago because the poem in which Mrs Eliot would live on forever got it just right.

And Mr Eliot? Catherine did meet him again, briefly. In 1939, a small production of *The Family Reunion*. Catherine played the young Mary, in whom she felt the presence of Miss Hale, the woman who waits, and waits. Mr Eliot had come all the way to Manchester to visit the cast. They were introduced one at a time, and, being the youngest, Catherine was the last to shake his hand. He showed no hint of recognition, and she never let on that they had, in fact, met before: she made no enquiries as to the welfare or otherwise of Miss Hale, made no mention of the book he signed for her one 'awkward' morning five years earlier in the town. When the handshake was complete (and his hand was as cold as she remembered), she stepped back and watched the rest of the cast ask eager questions and soak up his every word. Westminster Abbey on legs. She smiled inwardly. Did he enjoy the role of public monument? Or was it merely useful? A way of getting through the day? The talk, the eager questions from eager readers, the polite answers, all something for the public man to do while the private mind was elsewhere? He gave nothing away, and only once, at the end of his visit, did he give Catherine a sideways glance, almost conspiratorial, as if to say, 'Yes, I do remember you now,' and as if to further add, 'That's just between us.'

It was the most minute of glances and whether anything was really in it she will never know. Not that she would ever have betrayed the confidence of Miss Hale or intruded upon the private life of the public monument that had been so kind to come all this way for their little show. Nor would she have ever told him that she didn't really much like the play, that people didn't talk poetry, that he should stick to the printed page and leave the stage alone. (Years later she performed in the play again, this time as the older Agatha — detecting the sad formality of Miss Hale's conversation — and loved all that poetry she dismissed when she was young.)

Mr Eliot had stayed for an hour, patiently answering questions about the meaning of this and the meaning of that. Then, after tea and cakes, he had been escorted to the door by the director. And it was as they paused in the doorway that Catherine heard it, the booming laugh of the public monument, the laugh that told you that no matter how cold the shake of the hand may be, the heart was otherwise. How else could he possess such a laugh, the kind of laugh that turned heads and lifted the spirits of everybody in earshot? Then the laugh faded, he left, and Catherine never saw him or met him again. Nor did she ever know if Miss Hale came to visit again from faraway California, or if she still wore his ring.

And with that thought, Catherine now plunges her hand into her dress pocket and clasps the small tobacco tin with its contents that can surely be of no interest to anybody else. 'That's just between us,' his glance may very well have said. Did she return the glance with the most minute of nods? And did he see it and was he reassured? Perhaps. For years the tin lay buried in the bottom drawer of her chest in her old bedroom in the town. And amid the comings and goings, the films and stage shows and the travel to fabulous places, the living here and there, her marriages, her own 'special friends', she even managed to forget about it. Until her mother died in the early eighties and her things became Catherine's. And she simply thought to leave the tin there at the bottom of the chest, that is, until the wedding invitation arrived and she knew that Fate had stepped in and deemed the moment right for the thing to be returned to its proper place. Miss Hale and Mr Eliot were gone now, and the pact they made in the rose garden (sealed inside the tin) was no one's business but Miss Hale's and Mr Eliot's. And it is because it was no one's business but theirs that Catherine has never unfolded the piece of paper the tin contains and never read whatever is written on it. They are private words, a private testimony briefly exchanged years ago, and intended to be stored out of harm's reach, in a secret burial place away from the glare of the sun, the change of seasons and the passing of the years. Now the time was right for the thing to be returned to its proper spot in the garden. Where it had lain briefly before Daniel, in a long-ago, youthful prank, had claimed it for her.

With the children now fled from the foliage and the sounds of the wedding behind her, Catherine kneels by the edge of the rose garden and, with a stick picked up along the way, proceeds to dig a hole in the ground, deep enough to take the tin. And when the hole is prepared, she takes the tin from her pocket and consigns it to the earth, quickly filling in and smoothing over the surface with leaves and dry earth so as to create the impression that the ground has not been disturbed. And, as she does, she could swear that the roses, in the full glow of their second blooming, incline towards her, like old friends, welcoming back into the garden the things that are rightly theirs.

The task completed, she rises, brushes the dirt from her dress and hands, and turns to the marquee. The bride is calling to her, the children who had just before burst from the foliage are now running wild over the front lawns of the estate, and a photographer is organising everybody for a group shot. The young couple whose impetuosity has brought them all together are standing at the centre of the group, and as Catherine leaves behind the rose garden, she focuses on the young couple and her heart goes out to them, urging them on to happiness as she did all those years before when Miss Hale and her special friend made their visit to the house and exchanged confidences in that deeply private world of the rose garden.

The string quartet, hired for the occasion, strikes up, and the music is instantly, though faintly, familiar to Catherine. Throughout the photographs, the toasts, the talk and the laughter, it remains tantalisingly so. Now melancholic, now urgent, as though impatient with itself, until a flurry of sounds end with the jabbed, emphatic final note that signals the end of the movement, the end of the whole piece, the music slowly fading in the open air of the old estate, but never quite gone: at once still, yet still in motion; resolved, yet restless for more. Never quite done. And as she stares out over the lawns to the rose garden, Catherine pictures the old tobacco tin containing the remnants of the lost life and wonders if such things can ever be buried deep enough.

Acknowledgments

Many thanks to the following for their help during the writing of this novel:

To the Earl of Harrowby for showing me around Burnt Norton and for sharing his insights; to Max and Ailsa Scott for their generosity and kindness and for allowing me into Stamford House, Chipping Campden; and to Barry Kettle for showing me through the adjoining Stanley Cottage. Thanks also to Elizabeth Devas.

To Shona Martyn, Linda Funnell and Jo Butler at HarperCollins, and my agent Sonia Land (and all the gang at Sheil Land) for their support and enthusiasm.

Finally, my special thanks to my partner, Fiona Capp, for her constant support, suggestions and advice, not just in the writing of this novel, but all of them. And to Leo – the lion-hearted boy.